The Maltese Hunter

Paul Vincent Lee

The Maltese Hunter

Visit: www.paulvincentlee.com

A catalogue record for this book is available
from the British Library.

ISBN: 978-0-9572399-7-5

To Gail......for being an inspiration
&
ELD, as I keep my word

Author Note

In the summer of 2015, when I first thought of the main story line for this book; I had never heard of most of the people I then found myself researching.

As I did more research to help with my story, I got drawn more and more into the multitude of theories on just what happened on that fateful day in 1963 when US President Kennedy was assassinated. The well-known saying that "truth is stranger than fiction" has never been more appropriate than in this case.

"The Maltese Hunter" is fiction, but I have included as many verifiable facts as I could without being sued! I will admit from the outset that I have never believed in the 'Lone Gunman' explanation put forward by [the now totally discredited] Warren Commission; and I also accept that some of the conspiracy theories put forward are totally without substance, and only add to the difficulty of finding out what truly happened that day.

Although by writing this book; which I repeat is a work of fiction, I inevitably formed a view on who was responsible for the assassination, that view is not necessarily reflected in the storyline.

You don't have to agree with all, or indeed any, of the issues raised in the story……but I guarantee it will make you think.

No matter what; I hope you enjoy the book.

Paul Lee

Malta 2016

Acknowledgements

I would like to make special mention to Marlyn Cocozza whose financial assistance; over my earlier years as a struggling author, saved me from eating sand for my dinner. Thanks again Marlyn....and at no time did I really think you were involved in the JFK assassination.

***

I'm not thanking anyone else this time around....the usual names know who they are by now. If you don't know who they are.....buy "The Maltese Orphans" or "The Maltese Dahlia"......or both!

*

Paul Lee
Malta 2016

Table of Contents

Prologue

22nd Nov 1963
Dealey Plaza,
Dallas, Texas

Several shots ring out. The dream of Camelot is dead and; like King Arthur, it is impossible to separate the truth from the myth.

*

22nd Nov 1973
The Plaza,
Sliema, Malta

Josef Calleja was 40, over-weight & bald; and the few remaining teeth he had were an interesting array of colours, none of which were white. His job was drudgery; his marriage and children the same. He thought he had lost any degree of sex-appeal he may have had when he was younger; but the beautiful girl standing at the bus stop, smiling at his obvious frustration as he sat in his van; stuck in the early morning traffic heading into St Julians, made him think again.

She is hot. Don't I know her? Doesn't she live on Triq Ir Rudolfu, near Holy Trinity?

Josef Calleja leant over and wound down his side window......and t*en years after the death of one legend; another is re-born.*

*

22nd Nov 1983
The Trump Plaza, Atlantic City, New Jersey

Hank Restin: rags – to – riches; the epitome of the American Dream, holds a press conference announcing his Billion Dollar investment in a new casino strip in the city. Hundreds of people oowed and ahh-ed; clapped and cheered. A woman stands alone at the back of the auditorium. She doesn't have the dark, Latino look of her son; but she does have a fire in her eyes, and ice in her veins. After a few more minutes, she turns and walks out of the room; unnoticed by the fawning masses.

*

22nd Nov 1993

Pulizija Headquarters, Floriana Plaza, Valetta, Malta

A young Maltese girl; Thea Spiteri, achieves a life-long ambition and joins the Malta Police Force; il-Pulizija.

The end game begins.

Chapter One

Monday
23rd Nov 2015
The Blue Lagoon, Comino. 7.30 am.

The Blue Lagoon was red. Not all of it; just the area where the blood had formed an almost perfect circle around the bloated mass of what had once been a human being.

The first sun worshipers had arrived at the bay around 7.00 am; Superintendent Thea Spiteri of the Maltese Pulizija Homicide Squad touched down in a helicopter; 'commandeered' from the

Air Wing of the Armed Forces of Malta, at around 7.30 am. The sight of the mutilated body was her second shock of the still awakening day. Her first shock had been a proposal of marriage from Nicola Tizian; Malta's, never convicted; but the undisputed head, of the Corsican Mafia that had established itself on Malta over the previous decade or so......and her lover.

*

Spiteri stood on a small outcrop of rock next to where the lifeless body of a man was being pulled ashore by the two Responding Officers who had first attended the scene. She was flanked by DS Sarah Said and Inspector Raul Mifsud. Mifsud had been promoted into the position previously held by Spiteri before her promotion. He was a good Officer, Spiteri liked him; but there was obvious tension between Said and the man who was brought in 'over her head.' However, Spiteri knew that Said was dedicated and loyal, and it wasn't necessary to like fellow Officers in order to work with them. Said's feelings towards men in general, though mainly due to a spectacularly unsuccessful love life, was something that Spiteri was unaware of.

When Said pointed out a Pulizija launch homing-in on the beach, Spiteri looked out across the pristine waters of the lagoon. She quickly recognised Assistant Commissioner Grillo; the Senior Officer she would report to as he was responsible for Region B which included Gozo and Comino, and Magistrate Miriam Zammit. Magistrates always attended serious crime scenes, partly to offer advice, but also as an impartial witness. Spiteri was pleased that it was Zammit who had drawn this assignment. Zammit may have been 59 years old, and would be retiring the next year, but her mind was as sharp as any of her colleagues; and sharper than most. Spiteri knew that she would miss her. She had liked her ever since she had attended a court hearing many years previously, and heard Zammit thoroughly confuse a young Defending Avukat, by telling him to stop repeating himself when he had used the words: "prominent politician" and "liar" in the same sentence.

Like Spiteri, Zammit had never married and had no children; but the passage of time had not been kind to Magistrate Miriam Zammit. A once much sought after partner, even back in the days of 'proper courting procedures;' a combination of the vagaries of the Maltese sun; decades of study and long hours trying to establish her place in the macho-male legal establishment, and a love, bordering on obsession, for Zeppoli ta san

Guzepp, a sweet dish only the brave will attempt; had all contributed to Zammit appearing wizened rather than wise.

Assistant Commissioner Grillo walked over to where Spiteri and the others were standing: 'Another one?'

'Looks like it Sir' replied Mifsud for the group.

'OK, you know what to do. Get the body to the Morgue, dig out the bullet and get it sent to Ballistics….see if it's a match to the any of the others. Anybody have any idea who he is?'

'No, but half his head being missing doesn't help' said Spiteri.

'Suppose not. OK, let me know when you find out, Thea. Then get the family informed. The Press Conference is set for 4.00 pm; try & have as much info as possible by then.'

'Yes, will do.'

*

Jafar Nimeiri was freezing and close to death. He knew if it wasn't for his insulated and thermal clothing he would already be dead. The rubber dinghy he had been in; along with many others, had long since disappeared under the waves of an angry Mediterranean. So had all the other people; his fellow dreamers, who had been in the dinghy with him. He cried for the dead, and for the fact that he had cheated death…..and them. For now at least. Perhaps it was now Jafar's turn to die. Thoughts of his wife and child, waiting patiently for his return; and his friends who understood the importance of his journey, filled his head. But now Jafar Nimeiri doubted that his family and friends would even hear that his brave attempt at establishing a better future for them; had disappeared under an ocean of tears along with the hopes of countless others.

How different things had been 2 months earlier as Jafar had set out on a deliberately circuitous journey full of hope, determination…..and a love for his country and family that would sustain him through the difficult times that he knew lay ahead. Jafar finally crossed into Libya; his gateway to the West. Jafar had intended travelling to Tripoli but had found out through conversations with fellow travellers that he should avoid Tripoli and head for Zuwara. Even being put into a compound on his arrival on the outskirts of Zuwara; hadn't dampened Jafar's hopes that he was on the brink of achieving what he had set out to do.

After one week in the compound, Jafar, and thousands of others were directed to a dock in Zuwara and from there on to a ship…..a ship headed for Italy. Looking back at the heat hazed image of Zuwara as Jafar's Ark steamed out towards the blue horizon; Jafar saw the convoy of 6 or 8 small boats following along behind his ship but thought nothing of it. Not until his ship stopped. Shouts and confusion filled the air as the ship's crew; now armed, rounded up the passengers on to the deck. This was not supposed to happen; someone had messed-up; or taken 30 pieces of silver.

The flotilla of small boats that Jafar had seen soon drew alongside and had started throwing rubber dinghies into the water. Life became a blur for Jafar, as frenzied shoving and bursts of warning machine gun fire cowed the mass of humanity, forcing them down rope ladders and onto the dinghies. A satellite telephone was thrown into the dinghy as it was cast off from the small craft it had been tethered to: "carry on for another mile, then you'll be in Italian waters, call the Coast Guard, they will come and guide you into Sicily…..you will be free. Ciao." And with that; they were gone.

Jafar's dinghy stayed afloat for about 30 minutes before it started taking in water; after another 30 minutes, Jafar was floating alone in the watery expanse with only his God for company.

*

The Mists of Time
The Golden Age

Aeons had passed since time began. Gaia;
Mother Earth and Uranus; Father Sky had
been overthrown by their own children, and the
second generation of their descendants; The
Titans, now ruled the heavens. Atlas; son of
Lapetus, sat on Mount Othrys and looked
down with love upon his own child; Calypso.

Chapter Two

1985
Malta

Peter O'Toole had arrived in Marsascala in the March of 1985; and immediately fallen in love with the quiet fishing village. He had red hair & a slight Irish lilt to his speech. No-one was sure exactly what it was that he did for a living, but his tales of mischief in Erin; and 'knowing' wink when asked, as he often was: " Your father wasn't the Peter O'Toole was he?" : accompanied by his favoured reply: "Well now, it wasn't Lawrence of Arabia to be sure" ; made him a popular figure in the community. Peter settled in the small southern fishing port because it was "beautiful, quiet....and home to "Malachy's" Irish Bar." He was friendly and jovial but somehow remained a private man at the same time.

Although it was true that he had been born in Ireland and that his mother; Mary Burns, did indeed claim to be a childhood sweetheart of the famous actor, that was the extent of the connection. Mary Burns left Ireland for Scotland when Peter was two years old, and she was seventeen. Within a year, she had met & married a shipyard worker named Joe Dixon. By the time she was 21 she had had three more children....and had died at 43, having lived more than half her sad life as an unpaid servant and punch bag. Peter had left the troubled home several years earlier and joined the Merchant Navy. He was in Karachi when he heard of his mother's death. The telegram from Joe Dixon read: "Your Mum dead. Send money for funeral...I'm not paying it." J D.

By 1993, Peter O'Toole was regarded as happy and settled by those who knew him; others commented that he seemed odd, eccentric.....lonely. But none of those words truly described him. Peter O'Toole was lost. He was 40 years old and had been lost for 30 of those years.

The Maltese Hunter

He knew the years count exactly, as it was indelibly branded in his brain. His life had been changed forever when, as a child of 10, the man he longed to call 'Dad' had struck him so hard one night for saying he didn't want the dinner he was given; that his jaw was broken in two places. The overworked and underpaid staff at Glasgow's Royal Infirmary accepted the always popular, "he fell down the stairs" story, without comment. But being lost is not the same thing as being unable to function. A man castaway on a desert island, lost in the mountains or another wilderness, still knows that he must eat and drink; must have heat and shelter. He also learns that he must live alone. Other people can, and do, enter his life; but they exist on one plain….he on another. He can cross into their plain, but they cannot enter his. He had known a man once; a man who was completely paralysed and confined to a wheelchair. The man spent his whole life sitting in his chair at the bay window of his home, watching time; the seasons, children walking through life from primary school to University, work, children of their own. People from that world entered his home every day; nurses, home helps, social workers. They entered his home, but never his world. Peter O'Toole had forever considered that man a kindred spirit.

Peter O'Toole went missing in 1994; he was never seen again.

*

Two days prior to the body being found in the Blue Lagoon; an immaculately dressed chauffeur had been holding a car door open for his latest client. Hank Restin wasn't rich; he was 'filthy rich,' and loved letting people know it. His private jet had touched down at Malta International Airport, by Luqa, only five minutes before; and already he and his son, Jon, were in the back of a limousine and on their way to the Portomaso Hilton. Despite being the most prestigious hotel on the island, Hank Restin referred to it as 'the cock sticking out of the arse hole of the world.' He was not a great fan of the attractions of Malta; Las Vegas and Atlantic City being more in tune with his idea of culture. His wife, Helen, had just finished a month-long Mediterranean cruise with her sister, and their ship had docked in Valletta the previous day. His sister in law was already on the way to Malta airport to fly back to London; but Hank and his son would be joining Helen to continue the cruise, firstly around the Aegean Sea, before berthing in Sicily. However, they were going to spend a few days in Malta in order to allow Helen Restin to get her "land legs" back. Neither Hank nor Jon minded, as it would allow them to get a bit of solo flying done, and deal with a long-standing business issue that needed resolving. Both held Private Pilot Licences with Hank's being his proudest achievement in life; apart from making money.

Neither of the Restin men would go on the cruise.

*

Jafar Nimeiri wasn't freezing anymore. He wondered if he was dead. His fear prevented him from opening his eyes. He became aware that he wasn't bobbing up and down as he had been before. He felt a gentle prod on his side, heard some words he didn't understand. *Jafar, your ancestors were warriors; open your eyes.*

The salt and intense sunlight pierced his eyes. He heard the nervous laughter of two young boys running away along the beach from where he lay. Jafar Nimeiri didn't move, but he knew he was alive.

Chapter Three

Thea Spiteri sat at her desk in Pulizija H Q in Floriana and pondered over what looked to be the latest in a chain of gang / drug related killings. She pondered the cases in two guises; one as a Pulizija Superintendent; and also, with stomach-turning anxiety, as a woman agonising over whether her possible husband-to-be was involved in the killings. He had assured her that he was not, but still her doubt remained. *How can I even think of marrying a man who might be a killer?*

This latest killing would bring the body count to 10. *When I joined the Pulizija, 1 killing a year would have been considered a lot.* But now even the Press, who at first has expressed their "rage" at the killings, now merely reported them as another "tit-for-tat turf war killing" and sometimes didn't even do a follow-up report on the investigations; especially when 'No progress' was all the Pulizija Media Officer had to say. Once Spiteri found out the latest victim's name, she would find it simple enough to link him to the bloody chain:

"Is-Suldat attempts to kill Il-Lion – fails. Il-Lion gets Il-Haqqa to put a bomb under Is-Suldat's car – discovered. Il-Lion shot and killed. Fellow gang member Il-Yo-Yo – shot and killed. Il-Sudat is shot and killed. Il-Gilda – shot and killed. Il-Haqqa – shot and killed. Il-Kohnu shot – survives – but is arrested for attempted bank robbery. His assailant – shot and killed in his home."

Some in the Pulizija were of the opinion that they should just be left alone.....in the hope that they eliminated themselves....scenes like today's had Spiteri beginning to warm to the idea.

She sometimes found it strange not to be the hands-on investigator of a murder, but Mifsud and Said had to be allowed to tackle things in their own way, and Spiteri had to admit that she didn't miss the daily grind involved in fruitless lines of enquiry.

*

That same afternoon a man; who would come to be known as 'White Suit,' came off a scheduled Air Malta flight from London and went straight to the taxi booth tucked away in the right hand corner of the Malta Airport Arrival area. He paid his 20 euro fare for the trip to St Julians and got into the back seat of a white Mercedes.

'Do you know Nicola Tizian's bar in St Julians?' he asked the driver.

'Which one......he has many?'

'Which one of them will be the busiest at this time of the day, would you say?'

'Definitely 'The Black Bear.' '

'Take me there then.'

*

Like his lover, Thea Spiteri; Nicola Tizian was also pondering the day's events. He had agonised over asking Thea Spiteri to marry him; but he loved her, *surely that was enough; all that needed to be said?* He too was surprised about yet another murder taking place on the island; a murder he knew nothing about, and certainly never sanctioned. He sat on his regular stool in

The Black Bear watching the tourists pay inflated prices for average food and tried to make sense of the two events.

The man in the 'White Suit' who came into the bar carrying an attaché case couldn't have been more conspicuous if he had blown a trumpet at the same time. Tizian didn't feel uneasy but somehow felt that this stranger was looking for him. He glanced over at his two body guards; glad to see that they too were watching the new arrival warily. 'White Suit' walked straight up to the bar and beckoned one of the bar staff over: 'Excuse me, I'm looking for Mr Tizian, is he in today?'

'I'm Nicola Tizian.'

'White Suit' turned and offered his hand. 'Mr Tizian, I would like some of your time if that would be alright?'

'What's this about?'

'White Suit' looked around: 'Can we go somewhere more private?'

'What's this about?' repeated.

'It's a story I think you should know about; an unfinished story.'

'I'll give you 10 minutes' Tizian pointed to a corner 'over there….leave the case.'

Nicola Tizian and 'White Suit' were still talking 2 hours later. Nicola Tizian was crying.

*

'Raymond Sarstedt' said Mifsud.

'Our victim?' replied Said.

'Yes. Raymond Sarstedt. Born in USA, been living in Malta for the last year; 49 years old.'

'Employed?'

'Doesn't seem to be, but must have money given he has a penthouse in Pendergardens.'

'Nice.'

'Very.'

'Cause of death…..do I need to ask?'

'Nope….a single shot to the head.'

'Ballistics report in yet?'

'No, hopefully tomorrow. I wouldn't hold out too much hope there Sarah. The rest have been killed by a variety of guns, so……'

'Yes, you're right, let's just wait; we may be surprised.'

Sarah Said would never say a truer word in her whole Pulizija career.

*

Miriam Zammit had taken the opportunity, since she was already at Comino, to be dropped off in Gozo rather than be taken back to Malta. She had a small holiday razzett there that she had painstakingly restored over the years; with the intention of retiring there in time. Now that that 'time' had come, she was in two minds about how she felt about retirement. The law had been her life but, despite her best efforts, it was obvious that the islands were now more lawless than they were when she started out. She knew within herself that the basic culture of the islands had changed; drugs, technology, vice and unfettered immigration had all contributed to the 'modernisation'…..perhaps her 'time' had passed. Thoughts of drugs and crime turned her mind to Thea Spiteri. She liked Thea, admired and respected her; but couldn't fathom her taking-up with a known criminal. *What are you thinking Thea?*

Today's incident was just another example of the changes on the islands, and Zammit was glad that none of the cases would affect her. She doubted the same could be said for Thea Spiteri.

*

That evening Thea Spiteri sat on her couch, flicking through an old copy of "Pink"; Malta's foremost fashion magazine. She wasn't particularly interested in fashion, but she refused to watch the drivel that passed for TV viewing in Malta. She was glad to toss the magazine to the side when she heard Nicola Tizian coming in through the front door. Tizian walked over to the couch, leant over and kissed Spiteri on the forehead; before slumping into an armchair opposite.

'What's wrong?' Spiteri said.

'Why are you asking that?'

'You look as if you've seen a ghost.'

'Maybe not seen...........more a case of being enlightened.'

'What are you talking about Nicola?'

'Nothing; I'm OK. How was your day?'

'Apart from pulling a near headless man out of the sea.........pretty normal. Mind you, that sort of thing is becoming the norm these days.' Spiteri studied Tizian's face: *does this involve you Nicola?*

'I heard about that. Fucking fools.'

'Who are?'

'These jumped-up shoplifters who think they are big-time gangsters.'

'Like you, do you mean?'

'Not tonight, Thea.......not tonight.'

*

Jafar Nimeiri hadn't moved from the beach he had been washed up on. He would find out later that he was at a place called Ghar ix-Xagra; not far from Qrendi, but for now all he wanted was food and water, and to move through the darkness of the approaching night. Jafar started walking.

*

The Mists of Time

Like many men after him, Cronos; who had overthrown his own father, Uranus, was, in turn, overthrown by his own children. Among those children was the one who would become God of all Gods: Zeus.

Chapter Four

1980
The Azure Window
Gozo

Being a Saturday, the Car Park and coffee shop at Gozo's popular tourist attraction; the Azure Window, were both busy. The freedom the children enjoyed as they clambered over the rocks and ran down to the stony beach suited Martin Camilleri perfectly. All eyes were either glued to cameras, or enjoying the antics of the children; leaving none to see 17 year old French backpacker and exchange student, Maria Piaf, being enticed from the bus stop and into a red van with the lure of a quick journey back to the ferry terminal at Mgarr.

For the rest of their lives Maria's parents would never know if their daughter boarded the ferry or not.

***

Thursday

Three days had passed since the body of Raymond Sarstedt had been pulled from the Blue Lagoon. Mifsud and Said had learned all they could about the murder; which was 'not a lot.'

'Any word from ballistics yet, Sarah?'

'No, shall I call them?'

'No, I'm going to get Superintendent Spiteri involved.....ask her to read the riot act to them. It was supposed to be a priority. I don't think I carry enough clout to merit special treatment!'

'That will come. Next time you're in the Lab, punch one of them......works every time.'

Mifsud was pleased that the coolness between him and Said seemed to have passed; he was sure they would make a good team. Said wasn't sure she felt the same way: *he was a man after all.*

*

The previous few days may not have been that fruitful for Mifsud and Said; but Jafar Nimeiri felt that he had been blessed by God. It was true that he had felt guilt at having to steal food, and some clothes that had been hanging out to dry, but his need was great and he vowed to return and pay for the items.

Europe truly was the "Promised Land." Not only had Jafar found food and clothing in only a couple of days; but he had also found shelter.....and a job. And it was the perfect job. His meanderings had eventually brought him to the outskirts of Malta International Airport. There he had befriended another like-minded soul and although he was an Egyptian; Jafar knew enough of the language to be able to hold a basic conversation. His new friend had taken him to an outlying hanger at the airport, and informed him that this was where he, and 6 others, lived. They all had jobs as cleaners in the airport; and Jafar would be starting the next day. Jafar was overjoyed, even though he didn't intend staying too long.

*

Hank Restin was determined to get one last flight under his belt before he had to start preparing to leave Malta; and was at the Malta Flying School for 7.00 am. His hired, single engine; 2

seater Cessna 150, was primed and ready to take Hank away to a world where life's pressures lay far below him.

He was a little put-out that the arrangements had been changed at the last minute, and a bit surprised too at the courier, but he wasn't going to let anything interfere with the serenity he always found while dancing through the clouds. *Yea OK…..safety reasons….but what the fuck.*

*

'You can't find it! What the hell are you talking about?' Spiteri was on the phone to the ballistics people straight after Mifsud's request that she flexes her muscles with them.

'I'm sorry Superintendent, but we have spent a whole day and night looking for both the report and the bullet; we just can't trace them. I don't know what else to say, nothing like this has ever happened before.'

'You're sorry! I'm sorry, but that is just not good enough. You have one hour to call me back, and you better have that report. If not, I'm personally going to phone the new Pulizija Commissioner……and you know his views on incompetency……you'll all be looking for new jobs in the morning.'

Spiteri slammed the phone down; but something inside her told her that there was something more than an over-sight at play here.

She would be right about that.

*

That evening, Nicola Tizian picked up 'White Suit'. He was impressed with 'White Suit's' timing and accuracy. If he was being honest, he had thought that the plan was a bit mad when he heard it. Now though he nodded his admiration as 'White Suit' got into his passenger seat. *Wouldn't attempt it myself; but this guy is certainly something*

Chapter Five

1987
Mosta

John Rizzo just did not accept that anything he felt could be described as perverted. How could it be that for centuries the naked female form had been admired, adored even; by painters and sculptors, photographers and film makers, yet people frowned when he remarked on it and turned their noses up at the magazines and films he bought? Popes and Kings had paid fortunes to be able to gaze at such beauty, but it was "disgusting" for him to spend 10 euro!

But John Rizzo knew that his time had come and that he would soon be able to walk through Mosta with his head held high; because he, John Rizzo, was about to start dating the most beautiful girl to ever work in the Local Government offices where he himself worked.

It was true that Connie Fenech was a lot younger than him; but she always stopped to talk to him any time she passed the room that doubled as his 'office' and the cupboard where he kept his cleaning materials. She liked him, he knew she did, and he was going to ask her on a date that evening when they both finished up for the week-end.

Connie Fenech never turned up for work on the following Monday or, in fact, any day thereafter. Suspicion fell on John Rizzo, and his own disappearance a week or so later only added to the mystery.

Neither employee was ever seen again.

***

Officials from Malta's Bureau of Air Accident Investigation estimated that when Hank Restin's Cessna 150 crashed into fields just south of Bahrija, it was travelling at over 100 miles per hour. There was no obvious cause for the crash, which was usually the case at this early stage; and they confirmed that there was only one person on board; the pilot. His identity was established from his personal belongs, including his passport, and tablets found in his pocket indicated that Hank suffered from high blood pressure. Investigators surmised that a heart attack was a possible cause for the crash and made a note for the coroner to look for evidence of that during the Post Mortem.

Word of the crash had spread quickly, but Thea Spiteri didn't pay any special attention to the story, as she knew she wouldn't be involved in any investigation. Assistant Commissioner Grillo was about to change that.

'….but why? It's not my case, or even field!' said Spiteri as she sat across the table from the Assistant Commissioner.

'Thea, please, I know but listen. The victim, Hank Restin, is…was….a very influential person in USA. Millionaire investors, politicians, sports stars etc. The Commissioner doesn't want his wife and son to have to deal with Renato; he's a good officer, but tact isn't his strong point.'

'But I'm in the middle of a murder case!'

'How's that going? Any progress?'

'No.'

'You can spare a couple of hours then. Please meet the Restins at the Hilton tomorrow at 10.00 am tomorrow morning. Anything else?'

Spiteri considered bringing up the ballistics problem, but decided to leave it. *Get the babysitting over with first.*

The following morning, Thea Spiteri reluctantly made her way to the Hilton Hotel in Portomaso. On the way there, she called Mifsud.

'Raul, anything from Ballistics?'

'No Ma'am.'

'Right….I'm tied-up for the next hour or so. Once I'm free I'll go to the Ballistics Lab and get to the bottom of this. I'll keep you informed.'

'Right, Ma'am, I'll wait till I hear from you.'

Spiteri had no idea that she wouldn't need to go to Ballistics; Ballistics would come to her.

Helen Restin was immaculately dressed and walked with admirable poise into the foyer of the hotel; from the Lifts area behind the Reception desk. She greeted Spiteri in a polite and friendly fashion. She exhibited no signs of distress, but Spiteri could tell that she had recently been crying. Her son, Jon Restin, appeared calm and collected; though he too had obviously been crying. After Spiteri formally introduced herself;

emphasising, at Grillo's insistence, the fact that she was a 'Superintendent': all three moved to a quiet corner of the vast foyer.

'Has it been established yet how Hank died, Superintendent?' asked Mrs Restin.

'Not conclusively, but foul play has been virtually ruled out. A heart attack looks like the likely cause.'

'Mm…I always thought it would be a bullet.'

'Why do you say that?'

'Wealth brings enemies Superintendent……powerful enemies.'

'Has the plane been checked?' asked Jon, before his mother elaborated further.

'Again, not 100% completed, but the investigators are sure that there was no mechanical failure.'

'Or bomb?' said Helen Restin.

'Or bomb' replied Spiteri; wondering just who these people actually were.

Spiteri could see that despite her resolve; Helen Restin was toiling under the strain of her husband's death. After a few more minutes of general chat, Spiteri left the hotel, assuring the Restins that she would be in constant touch, and that they had to call her directly if they needed anything.

When Spiteri left; Helen Restin told her son that she was going to lie down. Jon stretched out on a couch and thought back to one of his favourite memories of his father. Jon knew of his father's love of flying; and as they headed out to the airport he sensed that his father was going to take him somewhere special in his plane, since it was his 21st birthday that day. But his father didn't take the normal route and they soon pulled up outside a Flying School: 'In you go son, it's all paid for; the owner is one of my connections; if you get my meaning. Put your mind into it and you'll have your PPL in no time and, once you have enough flying hours under your belt, you'll have your own plane too.' Jon Restin was delighted, having a Private Pilot Licence was one of his dreams; emulating his Dad in all things, his only desire.

*

Outside the hotel, Spiteri immediately focused on getting to the Ballistics Lab. Her mobile rang: it was the Commissioner's Office.

'Sir.'

'Superintendent, can you attend at my office immediately please?'

'Yes Sir, can you tell…….' The line had gone dead. Spiteri told her driver to get her to Floriana as quickly as possible; 'without killing me.'

Thea Spiteri had only met the new Commissioner; Commissioner George Malia, on the odd occasion in the few months since his appointment; so couldn't say that she 'knew' him, but she was impressed by his views on introducing change to the Pulizija. His crackdown on corruption seeing a Deputy Commissioner; two Assistant Commissioners and several Superintendents and Inspectors "head for the hills." Some of the names had surprised Spiteri, but she was happy they were gone if it meant that her beloved Pulizija was cleaning up its act.

As she approached the door to the Commissioner's Office, his Secretary motioned for her to knock and go straight in.

When Spiteri entered the Commissioner's Office she almost started to laugh but sensed that this was somehow a serious situation. Standing on the far side of the room were two men dressed in dark suits, wearing white shirts, black ties…..and sunglasses. Spiteri looked from the men to the Commissioner; he was motioning for her to sit down.

Spiteri complied, at the same time saying: 'I take it this is about Hank Restin?'

'No'

'No…..what then?'

Paul Vincent Lee

'Your boyfriend, Ma'am' uttered an American
drawl.

Chapter Six

1994
Marsascala Bay

Peter O'Toole knew that he'd had enough to drink. He had never been an aggressive drunk and when the "No more for me" time came, all he wanted was his bed.

O'Toole gestured goodbye to the staff in Malachy's and wandered out into the balmy evening for his nightly jig home. *Michael Flatley!! Michael fookin Flatley…..I'll fookin River Dance ye…..this is me Sea Dancin, Michael!* Peter O'Toole roared in laughter as his first "move" resulted in him falling against an upturned canoe sitting on the Bay's walkway. *Whit bestard poot that thir?* More laughter.

Peter O'Toole didn't feel the self-imposed scratches and bruises his journey home was inflicting as he approached the "Zest Nightclub" that sat on the corner of the street where he lived. *That's more like it; Travolta….fookin Travolta….* O'Toole was in the process of trying to remove his jacket in true "Saturday Night Fever" mode when he noticed a girl huddled up and crying in a doorway across from the club. Although he was drunk, O'Toole knew when someone was in distress. He walked over to the girl.

'Are you OK, wee Coleen.'

The girl looked up at O'Toole. Her eyes appeared glazed but O'Toole couldn't smell any alcohol.

'I just want to go home' she whispered.

'Of course, you do. Is your house far; will I organise a taxi for you? Don't worry about money, I'll pay it.'

'No, I live just at the top of the next street.'

O'Toole studied the girl's face for a moment; noticed her torn top: 'Do you want me to call the Pulizija?'

'No!'

'OK, OK….I'll walk you home then. Is that what you want?'

'Yes, please. Thank you.'

O'Toole saw the girl home safely, and 10 minutes later was gladly flopping onto his bed, murmuring: *fookin Travolta*.

The banging on his door confused O'Toole at first: *What time is it?*

'Open the door; Pulizija!'

O'Toole stumbled to the door and opened it: 'What's the…….' O'Toole never finished his question. He was spun around, handcuffed and in a Pulizija car before he had fully taken in what was happening. The following morning O'Toole realised that a night in a cell was the best way to sober up fast ever invented.

A court-appointed lawyer was telling him not to worry and that he was confident that O'Toole would get bail.

'Bail? What am I even doing here? What am I being charged with?'

'Rape.'

'What? There's some mistake.'

The next half hour passed in a blur as O'Toole was placed in front of a Magistrate, pled not guilty and, given that he had Maltese I.D and no criminal record, was granted bail.

Peter O'Toole stood in the bright morning sunshine outside the courthouse. *This can't be real, can't be happening. Am I dreaming…..have I gone mad?*

One week later, a tearful Evelyn Attard admitted to her parents and the Pulizija, that the 'old man' hadn't touched her. Her boyfriend had assaulted her, but she was too scared to tell her parents, so made the whole story up. When the Pulizija went to Peter O'Toole's house to tell him the good news….he was gone.

*

'How long has the body been here do you think?' asked Mifsud. He and a group of other officials were standing in a field just north of Naxxar, an hour or so after a farmer had uncovered some human bones.

The pathologist, Sharon Tanti, could only guess: 'I'd say 7 or 8 years, but I think I can tell you his name; his ID is still in his wallet, and so is some money.'

'Not a robbery then?'

'That's for you to decide Inspector. Anyway, his name appears to be Stephen Muscat. I'll get back to you once I've done the PM.'

'OK, thanks.'

Stephen Muscat's wife sat impassively as Said told her that remains had been found. She had reported him missing in 2001, and she still lived at the same address that she had shared with her husband before he had gone missing.

'I'm sorry to bring you distressing news, Mrs Muscat' said Sarah Said, as she and Mifsud sat down on a couch across the room from the stoic figure opposite.

'At least I know now that it wasn't another woman. Do you know what happened to him?'

'Not at this stage, but we will let you know.'

'Australia.'

'What?'

'Australia, that's where he dreamed of going; we talked about it a lot. At one time I thought he had fulfilled his dream and gone there......just not with me. Looks like I was wrong.'

*

Commissioner's Office
Floriana

'Does Nov 22nd, 1963 mean anything to you, Superintendent?' asked Blues Brother 1: Jack Carter.

'"Men in Black" was first released?'

A stoic stare was her reply. Commissioner Malia broke the silence: 'Superintendent......please.'

'Sorry. OK. Considering I wasn't born then......not a lot; no' said Spiteri.

'It means a lot to Americans......that's the day President Kennedy was assassinated.'

Thea Spiteri paused, unsure if she was following the correct train of thought: 'and.......?'

'.......and we think your boyfriend may be able to help us with that.'

'What! For Christ's sake......Nicola would have been one-year-old......is this a joke?'

'No joke, Ma'am. We're not saying he was involved.'

'Just what are you saying then?'

'We're saying he's involved now' said Blues Brother 2: Bill Clark.

'Now! In a murder that took place......what......50 odd years ago!'

'We understand that you are investigating the murder of a man whose body was pulled from the sea the other day?'

'That's right.'

'The bullet that killed your victim came from the same gun as the one that killed JFK.'

Spiteri stared at the two Agents; turned back to stare at the Commissioner, her thoughts churning in a vain attempt to make sense of what she was hearing.

'Again……is this a joke?'

'No, and we……'

'Wait a fucking minute! How do you know the ballistics results, we haven't even got them yet?'

'Thea, because of the "sensitive" nature of this issue, it is thought best that the report stays private' interrupted Commissioner Malia.

'That's not what I'm asking. How have you seen the fucking Ballistics Report and I haven't?' Spiteri paused, her mind still racing: 'Where is the bullet?'

'We have it in a safe place' said Clark.

'You have………! Look I demand to know what is happening here…..right fucking now.'

'Ma'am, I can see you're angry, I understand, but let me lay things out for you.'

'Yes…..that would be lovely……you "lay things out for me"….but talk slowly; I'm obviously just a confused housewife.'

'The CIA has the most powerful Internet presence in the world. Necessarily so, as we are the keepers of the peace.'

Spiteri sensed, but could not believe, what was coming next.

'In this role we have to monitor all Internet traffic, and flag everything and anything that impacts in any way with the Homeland. When your Ballistics Report was 'entered' on the system, it was copied to us. We saw the significance of course, 'took out' the information......and flew here to secure the site.'

'Wait....so let me get this straight. "Flag up, copied to you, you took out, secure the site": you are saying that you illegally monitor our system, interfere with it as you see fit and, presumably, break-in to a Pulizija Lab and steal evidence in a murder case?'

'Illegally is a moot point.'

Spiteri's mind immediately focused on a conversation she had once had with Nicola Tizian about what something "being legal" really meant. *Jesus Christ.....he's right.*

'Commissioner, you're not accepting this surely? Lock up these two cartoon characters and get the media in here, not to mention the Prime Minister.'

'Your Prime Minister is fully aware of the situation, Superintendent, and is co-operating fully with us.'

Spiteri stared at the Commissioner who, in turn, was staring out of his window.

Spiteri stood, but was unsteady on her feet: 'Fine, I'll go to the media myself.' Spiteri headed for the door.

'Superintendent, we appreciate that this will have come as a shock to you; but the fact remains that the gun that killed your victim, also killed our President. That is the only fact that matters. Should you attempt to interfere with our investigation in any way, you will be on the first plane off this island.'

'What the fuck are you......My God......you're actually threatening me with rendition....are you serious?'

'Perfectly.'

Spiteri again looked to the Commissioner for support; he was still looking out of his window. He spoke with his back to Spiteri: 'Thea, sit down, please. You have to co-operate with these men in any way you can. That is an order.'

A deflated Spiteri; at a loss for what to say or do, replied in barely a whisper: 'Order from who?'

'So, Superintendent......your boyfriend' said Carter.

*

Like his father; Jon Restin was an avid flyer and knew about plane maintenance and safety, and the normal causes of accidents. The Post Mortem on his father was 'inconclusive' but did state that his father's heart was "not good" and that he may have had an angina attack and not been able to properly control the plane when it went into a dive. The initial Air Accident Report was that the plane was in good order before the crash; the tragedy was as it seemed; a terrible accident.

Jon sat in the pilot's seat of a Cessna 150 similar to the one that his father had been in. He looked around the compact interior, contemplated for the first time that you really did take your life in your hands when you took to the air. But that was part of the appeal. Like his father, Jon too was surprised, and irritated by the time consuming 'safety' measures' that had been put in place at the airport; but after his father's death, he could understand them. He simply put it to the back of his mind, started the engine and taxied forward on the runway.

*

Raul Mifsud was surprised to hear from the Pathologist, Sharon Tanti, so quickly.

'I haven't done the PM yet, so can't say the cause of death for sure, but I thought I should let you know straight away that this man had been tortured before he died.'

'Right. How do you know?'

'Well, his toes have been cut off for a start.'

'It couldn't have been an industrial injury or his feet run over by something?'

'Not unless he was lying on the road.'

'Why do you say that?'

'His fingers are missing too...........and his teeth.'

'Right.......fuck.'

Mifsud asked Said to dig out the Missing Person Report on Stephen Muscat from 2001. It was obviously now a murder enquiry. He tried calling Spiteri several times, but with no success. *Corporate lunch no doubt.*

*

That evening Nicola Tizian, who couldn't seem to shake the habit of constantly referring to Pietru Massa as "White Suit' was thinking about how this man who within a few minutes of meeting him; had changed his life forever. So many thoughts had raced through his mind as this stranger recounted a story that Tizian instinctively knew was true, but a story that was so heart-breaking that it had reduced him to tears.

Tizian drove out to his arranged rendezvous point for picking up Massa; wondering if this man who he barely knew, yet owed so much to, would turn up.

*

Peter 'Red' O'Toole had befriended a rat. The first time it had come into his room it had bitten him, but now it took the scraps it was offered out of his hand. Peter had christened the rat: Ithaca. He spoke to it every day; it only replied sometimes. Peter didn't mind, he knew Ithaca was a very busy rat indeed.

Chapter Seven

Power, Revenge........and Christmas with friends.

The Mists of Time

Calypso, sea nymph, daughter of the Titan God, Atlas......watched as Odysseus begged for his freedom. Calypso, the concealer, ran her fingers over his bare chest; then turned and walked away.

Odysseus, castaway on a Mediterranean island on his way home from Troy, remained resolute; but knew that only the Gods could save him.

*

2015
Corradino Prison
Malta

Michael Grech was a worried man as he sat in his cell in the Corradino Correctional Facility in Paola, but perhaps not as worried as most men would be in his position. Facing his second rape charge in less than three years, he was confident that his 'friends' would, as before, ensure his freedom. His trial, like before, was going to be under Magistrate Zammit...*an old crone*....so he was wary since he knew that Zammit was incorruptible.....but *there is always a way, Michael.*

His victim, Adrianne Valletta, on the other hand, was convinced he would 'get off.' However, she too had secrets and knew that even if Grech did 'get off' in the courts; he would not 'get off' in life; *no man who crossed Adrianne Valletta ever had.*

*

Thea Spiteri was still in a state of numbness at what had just happened to her world in the last half hour but knew that she had to concentrate, fully take-in what was being said; her life would maybe depend on it.

'My boyfriend!…..what about him?……I told you…..he was only a baby in 1962.'

'We know, but please listen to what we are about to tell you. We hope that then you will be willing to help us; as a highly regarded Pulizija Officer, if nothing else.'

'"Highly regarded?"……doesn't feel that way' whispered Spiteri.

Commissioner Malia looked over to Spiteri: 'You are……I can assure you of that, Superintendent. All of us just have to deal with this situation and then, hopefully, move on.'

Spiteri nodded and turned her attention to Carter.

'Despite what you may have learned in school, Superintendent, or read over the years; President Kennedy was not killed by Lee Harvey Oswald. Yes, Oswald was in the Dallas Library Building, yes he did have a rifle…..yes, he fired a shot or two at the Presidential Cavalcade, but his nearest effort was probably closer to France than the President.'

'I don't understand; why was he arrested then?'

'He was a patsy, a sad individual with ideas of saving the world; who was easily 'recruited' by people who wanted to kill the President, and then offered up as a sacrificial lamb to the masses at the same time. People craved answers; someone to blame. Oswald craved fame and notoriety, a chance to air his views on TVs around the world. That was his motivation. The people pulling the strings, though, knew that that was never going to happen; his fate was already sealed.'

'He was killed wasn't he?'

'Yes, he was….by a man called Jack Ruby, who chose prison; with the promise of an early release date, over death.'

'What do you mean?'

'Jack Ruby was, as we say in the USA, a punk. A small-time hood with bad habits; the worst one being gambling. Unfortunately for him, he was as useless at gambling as he was at every-thing else. He owed the Mob a lot of money; he was given a choice: "kill Oswald, keep your mouth shut and your debt is paid…or….the back of your head will find itself many miles from your body in the next few minutes." He chose Option 1.'

'I still don't see what this has to do with Nicola.'

'President Kennedy was killed by two maybe three shooters; one of whom used the same gun that has just killed your latest murder victim.'

'But………'

'Two of the shooters were Corsican hit-men recruited by the Mob through their contacts in the heroine trade running out of Marseille at the time.'

'The French Connection.'

'Exactly.'

'And because Nicola is Corsican, you have assumed that he would know these people!'

'That……and the fact that the gun is here in Malta. All we are asking is that you find out what you can…..and pass it on to us.'

'And if I can't find out anything?'

'We will take your word. We are not trying to catch you, or even your boyfriend, out; we just need to see a 50-year investigation concluded.

Spiteri's nod was barely perceptible.

*

Adrianne Valletta wasn't young; but on a Friday night in "Hugo's" overlooking St George's Bay, she could compete with the best. Carefully applied make-up; modern hair style, plunging top and tight skirt……*bees to the honey pot.*

She was a little concerned that time seemed to be passing and she didn't want her schedule to be disrupted. Over the years, she had been faithful to her time-scale, and she knew that she had to factor in preparation time…..*don't worry Adrianne, someone will come. If not Grech, then someone….they always do.*

*

Prisoners are not allowed mobile phones in Corradino; and Michael Grech never broke the rules, model prisoner and pillar of the community as he was. Grech strolled to the Guard Station at the end of his corridor, 'I'll go for a smoke, 5 minutes Michael' said the guard.

Grech picked up the phone to receive his in-coming call: 'Hello George, nice to hear from you.'

Chapter Eight

2001
Naxxar

Stephen Muscat loved his wife; she was his first and only love. He just couldn't make love to her. Despite his patience and understanding, his wife's entrenched views that sex was dirty and something that had to be endured, had finally worn him down and he had decided to move on with that aspect of life.

He felt no guilt about his decision because his wife would be happy to be "left alone" and he would have the pleasure of living with his first love; along with the pleasures of Paceville. At least that was the situation up until he met Anna. Anna was fun, full of life…..and 15.

Stephen Muscat felt that his life was perfect. He went missing in October of 2001.

*

When Thea Spiteri had left the Commissioner's Office, she had called and left a message on Said's phone to say she was unwell and had gone straight home. Spiteri was still staggered by the morning's events and knew that she had to research the 1963 JFK killing, so she could have some idea of the background to what had led the investigation to Malta. She Googled 'JFK assassination'….and was staggered by the amount of information that was on offer. Spiteri realised that she couldn't possibly read her way through everything, and decided to concentrate on sites that contained a Corsican connection to the killing. Even after filtering the information down as much as she could; Spiteri was still overloaded with facts, fiction….and conspiracy theories. One thing she did find out was that the Corsican connection put forward by Carter was there….along with a hundred other theories. Fourteen hours after opening up her laptop, eyes closing, neck sore and brain shutting down in protest; Thea Spiteri staggered off to her bedroom. She was totally unaware that she would shortly be receiving help in finding her way through the JFK maze.

The following morning, she was still bewildered by the previous day's revelations; and had no idea how to deal with it. She found it impossible to believe that Nicola knew anything at all about the JFK killing, but she had to accept that the CIA twosome were right in enquiring about him when it came to anything to do with a Malta / Corsica matter. She decided to call him and suggest dinner; casually broach the subject in a 'general conversation' type way. *Fuck Thea, what are you saying…. "Oh yea, Nicola, remember that Kennedy guy that got shot 50 years ago; what do you know about it?"….Jesus wept.*

Her mobile rang and she saw that it was Mifsud. She knew he had tried to contact her all through the previous day, but saying: 'Sorry, I'm with the CIA' didn't seem like a good idea.

'Good morning, Raul. Sorry about yesterday, I was unwell.'

'I heard Ma'am, how are you feeling now?'

'Oh I'm fine….good night's sleep works wonders. What's happening, anything interesting going on?

'A lot actually. Number one: still no Ballistic Report on the Sarstedt killing. I'm beginning to think that……..'

'Raul, put that whole case on the back burner for the moment; other divisions are involved, that's all I can say…sorry.'

'Well, if you say so Ma'am.'

'What else?'

'A body has been dug up by a farmer. It's been there a while, 7 or 8 years the Pathologist thinks, it's definitely a murder enquiry, though; the victim, Stephen Muscat, had been tortured before he died.'

'Right, send all you have to date over to my office; I'll be in an hour. Anything else?'

'No Ma'am……well, I take it you know about Restin being killed in a plane crash?'

'I only missed one afternoon, Raul! I've already met with his wife and son.'

'Yes…..em…..but you do know that it's the son I'm talking about?'

'What?'

'Killed in a plane crash yesterday…..same as his father.'

*

The Maltese Hunter

Afternoon
Ramla Village
Gozo

The few inhabitants of Ramla were taken aback by the appearance of the strange man who had appeared in the village square; seemingly from nowhere. So off-putting was his appearance that some had gone back into their houses and locked their doors. Two women were on their knees on the pavement, close to this living scarecrow of a man, praying; another, of more practical beliefs, had phoned for an ambulance and the Pulizija.

The ambulance had arrived on the scene first; and a young Infermier approached the vagrant, just as he started to urinate where he stood. The vagrant's raucous laugh as he did so seemed to somehow ease the tension in the situation, but the two praying women had moved away at surprising speed.

'Bongu, can you tell me your name please?'
'86.'…..more laughter.
'Where are you from 86…..where do you live?'
'Down, far down.'…..no laughter.
'Are you hungry 86?'

'No food today. No, no.......not on a Thursday.'

'Well 86, I have good news for you, it's not Thursday today. Would you like to come with me and get something to eat........and a bath maybe?'

A radio was turned on in a nearby house. The man became agitated and swirled around as if being attacked from all sides.

'Sshh.....don't make a sound.'

'Don't you like the music 86?'

'No......I like soup...and togas....and red.'

*

That evening Thea Spiteri sat in the large foyer of the Portomaso Hilton, opposite the remarkably calm figure of Helen Restin. Spiteri had never married and had no children, but she couldn't imagine that if she had done, she would be so calm at both her husband and only son being killed within a week or so.

'Helen, I'm not going to be so insensitive as to ask you how you are; I can't begin to imagine, but is there anything, anything at all, you want to tell me?'

'Are you married, Superintendent?'

'No. I was close once, but no, never.'

'Unless you are very strong, you live your husband's life; not your own.'

'Was that a problem between you?'

'Not for Hank.'

'And you?'

Helen Restin glanced over at the huge swimming pool visible through the foyer's glass wall. She appeared lost in thought: 'it's all immaterial now, Superintendent.'

*

Chapter Nine

When Thea Spiteri entered the Commissioner's Office early the next morning she was again
tired and confused. After going to see Helen
Restin at the Hilton, she had spoken to everyone
she could regarding the crash that had killed Jon
Restin, and although it was still very early in the
investigation, she was assured that there were no
apparent signs of anything being wrong with the
plane; and that Jon Restin was a qualified pilot
who had flown Cessna 150's many times. She also
had it confirmed that he was alone in the plane.

She had spoken to Mifsud and Said and told them to concentrate on the two plane crashes. She reiterated that the Sarstedt murder was "Off Limits" for the moment and that Stephen Muscat had already waited 8 years: "so another couple of days wouldn't kill him." Neither Mifsud nor Said were quite sure if that was an attempt at humour or an unfortunate turn of phrase.

As she had expected, the two CIA operatives, Carter and Clark, were in the Commissioner's office when she arrived.

'Good morning, Superintendent' they said in unison. Spiteri merely nodded in their direction. *At least they're not wearing the sunglasses today.*

'Look, I haven't had time to speak to Nicola about this bullet thing. I've an 8-year-old murder and two suspicious plane crashes to look into and, to be honest; I have no idea how to even start a conversation with Nicola without raising suspicion' she said.

'We might be able to help you there' said Carter.

'Oh.'

'Yes, your victim, Sarstedt.'

'What about him?'

'He was an American citizen.'

'We're aware of that. I don't see that……'

'His father was from Corsica' said Carter.

'We think' added Clark.

'You think?'

'His father's name was Lucien Sarti.'

'And.........?'

'Sarti is one of the names high on the list of probable shooters of JFK.'

Spiteri had a vague recollection of the name from her previous night's studies: 'How many names on the list?'

'Not many.'

'OK, so what's the theory here? Sarti Snr shot Kennedy. His son 'inherited' the gun; someone somehow got the gun, and killed Sarti Jnr with it?'

'We don't know; that's why we're here.'

'Is Sarti Snr dead?'

'Yes, stabbed in a brothel in Marseille in 1985.'

'Nice. Probably bumped into a couple of the Kennedy clan in there too.'

'We don't appreciate that kind of humour, Superintendent.'

'No, I don't suppose you do.'

*

Despite themselves, the nursing staff in Mater Dei who had been assigned to care for "86" couldn't help but laugh at, and along with, their patient. The more unpleasant duties of washing; de-lousing; removing maggots and puncturing abscesses and putrid boils on his body were over; patient "86" was sitting up in a crisp, white T-shirt and apparently enjoying the attention of the staff, although suddenly, and without warning, he would retreat into a world of pain, and weep uncontrollably over "the others."

*

Raul Mifsud sensed the tension between himself and Said. He didn't feel that he was responsible for it per se, but he did feel that he should try to clear the air as much as possible.

Sarah Said was on the point of refusing Mifsud's unexpected suggestion that they go for a pizza when he added: 'we can discuss what's going on.' After the pizza, I'm getting a taxi home, so I'm having wine and brandy and anything else that takes my fancy..............and you can't stop me !'

'I wouldn't dream of it, besides, I might join you.'

'Great, but before you do; tell me, why don't you like me?'

'Who says I don't?'

'Me.'

'Ah.'

'Ah......that's it......Ah!'

Said appreciated Mifsud's light-hearted approach: 'let's chat over that wine.'

Mifsud and Said strolled through the new City Gate that has courted so much controversy; and over to Triq San Marku and settled down in a small bistro popular with locals. They ordered their wine first and agreed to share a pizza and local salad. Mifsud wasted no time getting to the point: 'So Sarah….horrible man that I am….how can I win you over!'

'I don't dislike you, Raul…….but change is difficult in any team…..it will be OK I'm sure.'

'There's been quite a lot of change in recent years I understand.'

'You could describe it that way. Murder, suicide and cowboy shows have all been part of the scene.'

'I heard.'

'Go on……I can tell you want to ask.'

'I heard that you were possibly part of the cowboy show.'

'"Annie Get Your Gun" you mean? No, I'm only teasing. Yes, one of the team left to follow his dream; and yes, we were romantically involved.'

'And now?'

'Now…..nothing.'

'I'm sure you'll have no difficulty finding another admirer Sarah.'

'I'm just not interested Raul; so if you were thinking of spiriting me away to a Caribbean island to wed as the sun goes down on a beautiful beach…..then sorry…..no can do.'

'Damn, I've bought the tickets as well!'

'Well maybe just for a holiday then! What about you, are you in a relationship?'

'Nothing serious. The job makes it difficult I feel.'

'That's true. No, I've had my share of being hurt; it's my turn now to be in charge.'

On her way home after the meal, Sarah Said admitted to herself for the first time, that it was neither Mifsud nor any man, that she longed for…..other to hurt them the way they had hurt her…..it was Thea Spiteri.

*

Adrianne Valletta threw her stiletto heels into the corner of her bedroom: 'Shit.' Her date for the night had looked promising at one time, but had turned out to be a perfect gentleman, and Adrianne was livid. *Where are you hiding Mr 2016?*

Chapter Ten

2008
Sweigi

Ramon Pace had an excellent relationship with his neighbour in Sweigi. Phyllis Brown was a retired English woman who had worked as an Admin Officer for the British Army and had decided to stay on living on the enchanting island that she had fallen in love with after the British withdrew for good in the March of 1979.

She considered herself to be very lucky to have Ramon Pace as a neighbour as he was always on hand to help her with anything she might need and, as a way of showing her gratitude, she made Ramon his lunch once a week.

Phyllis Brown's violated body was found one Saturday morning by a friend who had come to take her for a drive and, when she got no reply at the door, had called il-Pulizija.

Ramon Pace, like all the neighbours, was questioned over the murder, but no concrete suspicion fell on him.

Until he went missing.

***

Thea Spiteri decided to call Nicola Tizian as soon as she had made her excuses and left the Commissioner's office. She wanted to check that he was going to be free that evening. She wanted to be sure she was prepared for trying to catch-out her lover; and, at the same time, terrified that she might.

'Hi, Nicola. Are you available tonight? I thought you could come over to mine; I'll cook.'

'I'm always available for you Mrs Tizian!'

'Well, maybe that is one of the things we can talk about.'

'Then I shall ride in on my white stallion and sweep my Princess off her feet!'

'Fine……and after you've done that…..come to mine for 8.00pm.' She didn't wait for a reply.

The Maltese Hunter

Former Pulizija Commissioner Kevin Galea had been a friend and mentor to Thea Spiteri for most of his career before retiring. Spiteri needed advice, maybe a spot of counselling, and instinctively knew that Galea was the man to speak to. She had made an appointment to meet him in his Pembroke home that afternoon. "Of course, it will be lovely to see you, Thea. You can join me on my daily walk to Madliena Tower." The suggestion had cut through her like a hot knife. She was going to discuss marriage with one man, at the spot where another man had proposed to her. A proposal that; unlike the present one, she had said 'Yes' to straight away. *That was another life Thea…..you must move on.*

Kevin Galea was waiting outside his home as Spiteri drew up. She knew she couldn't talk about the CIA involvement, but there were so many tales surrounding Nicola Tizian that she knew she didn't need to bring up the present one. Galea greeted her with a smile and light kiss on either cheek.

'So, how are things, Thea?' he said as they strolled over to the rugged expanse that separated the sea from the start of Pembroke. It always amused Spiteri that the ground there was deemed a Heritage Park due to certain fauna only being found there; and was also the sight of the Maltese Army shooting range: *one way to deal with the tourists I suppose:* she smiled to herself.

'Complicated' she replied.

'I thought so. The life of a Superintendent is different to life as an Inspector, is it not?'

'It would seem so, Kevin. But that is not why I am here.'

'Oh, then tell me.'

'Nicola Tizian has asked me to marry him.'

'Ah…..and what was your reply?'

'I haven't replied…..yet.'

'Do you love him?'

'I love what I think he is.'

'But……'

'You know as well as anyone, Kevin. He has a certain reputation.'

'Have you experienced or witnessed any of these rumours?'

'No, but I deliberately do not have anything to do with his work life.'

'Thea, do you think he loves you?'

'Yes.'

'Do you think he is in any way a criminal?'

'What is a criminal, Kevin? Someone who breaks a law; a law that in another time or place is not a law? Sell marijuana in any state in America last year…..you go to prison for twenty years. Now…..you have a shop on the High St. and are up for "Business Man of the Year." And that will be the case here too, in time.'

'Maybe, but it is not the case now. Thea, are you telling me that Nicola is a drug dealer?'

'No, like I said, I completely distance myself from his businesses…….it's just that I can't completely get the doubts out of my mind.'

'Would you marry him if you weren't a Pulizija officer?'

'I think so, yes.'

'Then there is your choice. Choose wisely, Thea.'

Periods of silence and fragmented small talk filled up the next 15 minutes before Spiteri looked around to see where they were.

Thankfully for Spiteri, Galea had taken a different, shorter path than the one that leads to the Tower; and she realised that they were back at the start of the road where Galea lived.

'Would you like to come in for a coffee, Thea?'

'No….thank you, Kevin….there are dead bodies waiting for me!'

'Oh, the joy!'

Spiteri opened her car door and Galea gave her hug: 'Thea, one last thing to consider.'

'What?'

'Speaking to a lawyer.'

'Why?'

'What would your legal position; as a Pulizija Superintendent…..and a wife…..be?'

'For example?'

'Could you testify against him in court?

*

Raul Mifsud and Sarah Said didn't regret going for dinner the previous night, but their heads did. Raul had pulled into a space reserved for visitors to Luqa Airport: 'just let me go and get a bottle of water, Raul, sorry Inspector……or my head may well explode.'

'Get me one too please, I'll wait here, I'm not sure I could walk to the Terminal anyway without medical aid.'

Both Mifsud and Said sipped their water slowly and sat in silence for 10 minutes praying hopefully that the water contained some mystery ingredient that removed all pain.

Half an hour later they returned to the car after having spoken to some Maintenance and Plane Hire personnel.

'I'm not really sure what it is we are looking for, to be honest' said Said.

'Yea, I know what you mean but I don't think that there is a police officer anywhere in the world who believes in coincidence. Spiteri will be no different, and it does seem unlikely: two plane crashes, two related victims, no explanation for either crash. OK, the first is down as probable heart attack, but the second? Maybe we should check out everyone with a pilot's licence on the island; there can't be that many.'

'But why….the planes weren't landed safely by a "mystery man." Both the pilots were also the victims and the only people on board, and both were killed.'

'I know but there has to be some link.'

'I have a theory.'

'OK…..go.'

'The son apparently idolised his father. He goes up in a plane, seeks out the rough site where his father died…..joins him.'

'You mean he committed suicide?'

'Yes.'

'It's as good a theory as any, Sarah. We'll head back; I'll put it to Spiteri.'

*

When Michael Grech raped Adrianne Valletta at a Christmas Party in 2014, it was the second time in her life that she had been raped. It was not Michael Grech's second rape.

Adrianne Valletta had been raped as a teen-ager on her way to school; the bus had been late, and she foolishly accepted a lift in a van. She had told no-one of her ordeal, but neither did she forgive ….or forget. She lived by the motto: *Revenge is a dish best served cold.* She never married or had children but instead dedicated herself to weeding out men who had no right to be men, husbands or fathers; and ensured that they never were.

Michael Grech's trial for the rape had been re-scheduled for Monday 11th Jan 2016 in order not to be disrupted by the Christmas break. Michael Grech was a little peeved about missing out on the: "*hunting season" of office Christmas parties; a very fruitful time*: but consoled himself in knowing that he would not be found guilty of his crimes. He did not realise that he already had been.

*

Spiteri listened intently as Mifsud put forward the case for Jon Restin's death not being an accident per se, but a sad case of overwhelming grief resulting in suicide. She had already spoken again to the Air Accident people, who had confirmed that there was no mechanical failure or signs of a fatal 'bird strike' or anything of that nature.

'Raul, I'm going to go to the Hilton, to speak to Mrs Restin. I'll try and see if suicide could be a possibility.'

'How will you go about that?'

'With difficulty.'

Half an hour later, Spiteri walked into the foyer of the hotel and saw Helen Restin sitting alone in a corner of the expansive layout.

'Hello, Helen. Mind if I join you?'

'No, please do, I don't know anyone else here now.'

'I'm so sorry Helen; it must be terrible for you. When are you going home?'

'I'm not sure. Organising getting the bodies back to the States is a bit of a nightmare, especially with the holidays about to start. I'm not sure that I wouldn't rather stay here, to be honest; take the bodies back in January…..it's not as if there will be much celebrating being done at home.'

'Why don't you then? I'm assuming cost won't be a consideration.'

'No, it's not money; it's more a case of me wanting to be in a "home" not a hotel.'

Before she had put much thought into it, Spiteri made an offer.

'Helen, my partner is involved in the licensed trade, Christmas is a very busy time for him, we won't see each other much over of this period; why don't you come and stay with me? I'd enjoy the company.'

'Are you sure?'

'Absolutely. That's settled then. I'll just have to work a few things out first around shifts and things and I'll get back to you.

'Thank you, Thea….that is very kind of you. Any word on Jon?'

'Nothing definitive, Helen, but…….'

'But?'

'It's been muted that suicide, due to Jon being grief-stricken, might be a possibility.'

Helen Restin stared out at the pool: 'he retreated into himself when he heard about his father; it's possible.'

'Nothing is certain, Helen…..concentrate on the good times; the happy times. I have to go now, sorry; but it's a 'Last Supper' with my partner before the Christmas madness.'

*

Nicola Tizian was late arriving for dinner with Spiteri, but she was so used to his atrocious time-keeping that she smiled; as she considered his 8.15 pm arrival as a compliment.

'What?'

'Nothing. Are you hungry?'

'I'm always hungry for your cooking, Thea.'

'Smooth talker.'

'No, just a man in love!'

'Go and sit at the table.'

After a bowl of Soppa Tal- Xghir, a kind of barley broth, Spiteri had made a special effort to please the enigma of a man sitting opposite her.

'No…..it can't be! How did you manage it? Civet de Sanglier!'

Arguably, the signature dish of Corsica; Civet de Sanglier is a rich, casserole made with boar meat, mixed with onions, carrots, garlic, chestnuts and fennel.

'Thea, you have excelled yourself; thank you.'

'Well, I knew we wouldn't see much of each other over the next week or two; so I thought I'd make this special.'

The lovers enjoyed their meal, and their wine, mostly in silence; both just savouring the moment.

'Nicola, we were having a debate in the office today. What would you say was biggest news story of the 20th Century?'

'Interesting…… hard to say. Probably man landing on the moon.'

Spiteri watched closely for a reaction: 'What about the Kennedy assassination? Besides, some intelligent people don't believe the man on the moon story!'

'That is true, but no intelligent people believe the 'Lone Killer' story about JFK.'

Spiteri blanched: 'Why do you say that?'

'Why?.......because it is obviously not true! A little weed of a man, borderline retarded, completely without help or an accomplice, manages to assassinate the US President. It's just not possible!'

'Who do you think was responsible then?'

'The establishment, of course.'

'But why would they?'

'Everyone in a powerful position at the time hated Kennedy and his brother, Robert. Hoover at the FBI, Hoffa at the Teamsters, Richard Nixon and his gang, the CIA, wealthy Jews......they all hated the Kennedys for their crackdowns on the powerful organisations these kinds of guys were running.'

'What about.....and don't go all moody, Nicola......the Mob?'

'Yes, of course. But remember our many discussions around right and wrong; legal and illegal?'

'Yes.'

'Old Man Kennedy was a gangster, a mobster, a Prohibition Buster....whatever you want to call him. The bottom line is that JFK's father; Joe Kennedy, had the brains to court respectability; most of his contemporaries were just idiots. Rich.....yes...but idiots just the same. Just look at Capone.'

'You're not comparing Kennedy Snr to Capone surely!'

'Why not……liquor, molasses, gambling…..it's how they both made their fortunes.'

Spiteri felt that Tizian was getting a little agitated about the subject and decided to move on: 'well it's just as well it was all a long time ago.'

*

Red O'Toole didn't know how or why, but he knew things had changed. There had been no singing and no music for two days. Ithaca had cut his visits down to once every two days as well, but Peter O'Toole didn't question the friendship; it was agreed that Ithaca would visit when he could. He was, after all, a very busy rat indeed.

The broken men never knew the names of the songs or the music they heard. They only knew it meant terror was on its way. Some had died, some had gone mad; none were the men they used to be. The only constant in their lives was fear. Fear of silence and fear of noise; but most of all, fear of the ghost, the apparition…..The Priestess of Pain.

Ramon Pace heard, as always, the song……before the apparition appeared. Would she visit him…..or would someone else cry out tonight? He heard a key turning in a lock. The singing stopped, the screaming started. Ramon Pace thanked his God as tears of relief rolled down his cheek. He knew it would be his turn again soon enough.

Paul Vincent Lee

He had to get away...but how....he didn't even know where he was.

Chapter Eleven

When her mobile rang at 8.00 am the next morning, Spiteri noticed that there was no indication on her screen to show who the caller was. She considered ignoring it: *probably GO TV trying to get me to upgrade:* but she answered: *just in case.* Spiteri did not recognise the voice, but she would learn to.

'Miss Spiteri?'

'Superintendent Spiteri: who is this?'

'I prefer informality, so much nicer.'

'I had better warn you right now that I am a Superintendent in the Pulizija. Who are you…..what do you want?'

'I know exactly who you are Thea, and your rank, and your phone number……obviously!'

'I'm going to have this call traced.'

'Ha….I doubt that very much.'

'I will ask one last time: who are you?'

'Do you remember the Watergate scandal in America? It brought down President Nixon.'

'Not really.'

'Research it. You will find that the whole affair was brought down by one man; a man known only as "Deep Throat." '

'Are you suggestion that is who you are?'

'Oh no, no, no…..I'm much too young, Thea.'

'Why are you calling me?'

'I believe you are working in conjunction with the CIA at the moment.'

Spiteri couldn't believe her ears: 'Who told you that?'

'Ah, that would be telling. Look into Watergate. I'll call you soon.'

'But……'

*

Thea Spiteri had never been "big" on Christmas. For some reason she did feel compelled to attend Midnight Mass on Christmas Eve; work permitting, but she always felt it was fairer if the officers with children had that period off; and had often swapped shifts to accommodate them: all the more reason for her to feel a little resentful now that some of those people were clearly avoiding her. She had been enjoying her evening sitting at home with Helen Restin and would happily have stayed there, but felt obliged to attend the " 2015-16 Pulizija Christmas & New Year / New Beginning Bash" organised by the new Commissioner. No-one had actually been rude to her, but it was clear that her relationship with Nicola Tizian made people wary of being seen as "close" to her; although Spiteri was sure that some of those self-same people would have had more to hide than her. Spiteri decided to do a minimum amount of mingling and then discreetly leave: *but a large brandy required first Thea.*

A few people she did not know had congregated at the bar, but they all seemed to have been served and Spiteri managed to get through to the bar after a couple of polite 'Excuse me.'

'Yea, it's really odd. A shame obviously but the guy is really funny at times, the next minute he's in tears. I've checked our 'Missing Persons' list, even tried to see if anyone on holiday had been reported missing......nothing. I don't really know what else to do. Maybe he'll become a bit more lucid in time; at the moment all he does is smile inanely, talk gibberish about togas, music and ghosts to the male nurses.....he absolutely refuses to let female nurses near him.....goes mad if they try....but he eats like there's no tomorrow.....and, oh yea, talks about the colour red all the time.....keeps saying he's going to get him.' The group went to move off but Spiteri interrupted: 'Excuse me, I'm Superintendent Spiteri, can we have a quiet word?'

The young constable appeared flustered, wondered if he was in trouble: 'Yes, of course, Ma'am.' Not knowing what else to do he put out his hand: 'PC John Dawson.' Spiteri shook his hand, smiling inwardly at the obvious relief on the young constable's face: 'let's take a seat over there.'

Once seated, Spiteri asked about the young man's surname: 'My father is Scottish Ma'am, from a place called Glasgow. Have you ever been there?'

'Never, John..............I'm very sorry to say. John Dawson appeared a little confused by the answer but didn't have time to dwell on it. 'Look,

I overheard your story about the man who seems to have lost his mind. Tell me more.'

Dawson related all he knew but admitted that it wasn't much.

'Do you think you have gained his trust?'

'Yes, I would say so.'

'Do you think you could get him to talk to me?'

'I'm not sure; he doesn't seem to want female nurses or doctors near him.'

'Can we try in a couple of days' time?'

'Yes, of course. Can I ask why you are interested?'

'Years ago, I was involved in investigating a Missing Persons case. The missing man's name was Peter O'Toole, but he was known as "Red." '

'And you think this could be the Red my guy is talking about?'

'Who knows, but I have to try; my Red was never found.'

*

Christmas Day came and went, and Spiteri was glad that she had asked Helen Restin to stay. They exchanged small gifts, watched TV and drank wine, but most of all they were company for each other. Thea Spiteri was unsure who it was that needed the company more. Despite her unease, she had read up on the Watergate scandal and concluded that she had no idea what possible relevance it had to anything she was working on.

On the morning of Monday 28th Dec; her phone rang.

'Superintendent, it's Commissioner Malia.'

'Good morning Commissioner.'

'Good morning, I hope you are enjoying the holidays. I'm just calling to say that our two American friends have gone back to the States, but they will be back in January. In the meantime, and I haven't told them this yet, but I will have to when they come back; I've been shown evidence that your, eh, friend did know the victim Sarstedt. They had formed a company together a couple of years back, but it never traded. Still…..'

'Right, thank you for telling me Commissioner; I'll look into that.'

Spiteri had only turned her back on the phone when it rang again.

'Hello.'

'Hello to you my Princess!'

'Nicola, how are you?'

'Busy…..but never too busy to think of my love.'

'Such a charmer.'

'Seriously Thea, I feel bad about you being on your own at this time. Feel free to pop into the

Black Bear anytime, although I cannot guarantee you my undivided attention for long I'm afraid.'

'I'm not alone actually. I meant to tell you that I have a girlfriend staying over for a few days; it's been nice.'

'Really....that's good....what is her....For God's Sake, Henri.....not in there. Sorry Thea, I'll need to go....I'm surrounded by morons.'

'Bye Nicola.'

Once again, Spiteri had only replaced the phone in its cradle when it rang again.

'Thea, Miriam Zammit calling.'

'Miriam, how nice to hear from you; I hope it's not a problem with a case.'

'No, no....nothing like that. I'm just calling to wish you a belated Happy Christmas, and to suggest we meet for lunch one day. I'm going to be a lady of leisure shortly, so I'm putting my lunch victims list together!'

'I'd be delighted to be on the list Miriam; we can gossip about the Commissioner and all the other Magistrates!'

'Yes indeed, sounds wonderful. I have one more case to do, that disgusting man Grech, and then it's salsa, swimming and the classics for me! I'll call you.'

'Yes do that Miriam; I shall look forward to 2016: the year of the lunches! Bye.'

'You're a popular lady, Thea' Helen Restin called through from the living room.

'I think it's my charm and charisma.'

'Yes that could be it, or your Guardian Angel is watching out for you!'

Spiteri walked through into the lounge.

'I'm not sure I believe in them actually.'

'We all need angels, Thea.'

'You are a believer I take it?'

'What is a believer? We all believe in doing what is right.'

'Mm, it's just a pity we all can't agree on what 'right' is.'

'Ha, yes that is a problem! Maybe if the angels protect you; then what you are doing is right.'

Spiteri's questioning nature momentarily tempted her to ask about Hank and Jon's angels; but she quickly saw sense: 'Maybe; but all religions seem to profess that they are governed by love, and have a common goal; so why can't you all just love each other and chat about things instead of killing one another.'

'Sometimes we do.'

'Well then.'

'Well, what?'

'Why only sometimes?'

'Thea, sometimes you have to sup with the devil in order to thwart his plans.'

Spiteri recalled the many conversations that she had had with Nicola Tizian; his views on right and wrong. She shrugged: 'Helen, I have to go out now to see someone concerning a Missing Person case. Do you want me to drop you anywhere, or are you happy to stay here?'

'Oh definitely to stay here; don't forget I have the hire car should I change my mind later.'

'OK…..I'll see you later.'

Half an hour later; Spiteri was standing a foot or so behind Dawson as he spoke to '86' who was sitting beside his bed in the St Agnes Care Home that he had been sent to: 'A very good friend of mine is here to see you 86. She's not a nurse or anything; she just wants to talk to you. I'll be here all the time. She thinks she knows a friend of yours; 'Red.'

86 eyes opened wide: 'Red?'

Spiteri stepped forward. 'Hello, 86…..yes, I think I know Red too. Do you know where he is?'

'Red is in the kitchen. Oh yes, Red is in the kitchen.'

'Is he cooking?'

'Peter's not in the kitchen. No, no, no…..Peter is at the bar; he's not in the kitchen.'

86 starts to shake ….he curls up……screams.

'She's coming…..she's coming…..I hear her……I hear the music.'

'Who's coming, who is "She"?'

86 whispers: 'It's OK; she's going to the wine cellar. The screaming will start soon. Not me, no no no….I'm a good boy now…….poor Stephen.'

Walking back to her car; Spiteri got onto her mobile and called Said. 'Sarah I want you to compile a list of all reported missing men from over the last 30 years; whether they eventually turned up or not, but highlight the ones who didn't. I know 30 years sounds a long time, but it won't be that many names I don't think, and you can just do a Print-Out from the files of the names, I don't need details at this point.'

'OK. Will I email it to you?'

'No, I'm working on a few things at the moment. Let's all meet up on Monday 4th Jan. That gets all the holidays out of the way, and even gives you time to recover from your over-indulgencies!'

'Huh, chance would be a fine thing.'

'No male friends on your radar then?'

'No, not interested....well not in a boyfriend as such. There is someone I love, though.'

'Mm, I'll need to think about that one, Sarah. Anyway, 11.00 on Mon 4th....OK'

'Yes OK......see you then.'

*

On a whim, Spiteri decided to take a detour down to St Julians on her way back from her visit to 86 and take Nicola Tizian up on his offer of dropping in to see him. She parked up near one of her favourite restaurants; 'The Gozitan', and wandered around the corner to the Black Bear. She heard Nicola before she saw him.

Tizian was standing at the bar, arm around the shoulder of a man Spiteri didn't recognise; obviously slightly drunk and declaring to the world about how happy he was seeing his "Corsican Brother." Spiteri decided not to interrupt and turned to leave.

'Hello, Thea, aren't you staying?' it was Henri, the much-maligned manager.

'Not today Henri; it looks like a "Men Only" occasion!'

'Ah yes, an old friend of Nicola's apparently; from the USA.'

'Really, what is his name?'

'Pietru, Pietru Massa.....originally from Corsica......they were neighbours as boys I think. He's staying with Nicola for a few days I believe.'

Spiteri made her way back to the car deep in thought: *Strange that Nicola never mentioned he had a friend staying; especially when I mentioned mine. Still, maybe best that you don't know, Thea!*

*

Ulysses longed for the day that he could return to Ithaca and once again lie with his beloved wife, Penelope. He longed to see his children; to tell the people of his journeys. But he could not. Calypso revelled in the knowledge that Ulysses was hers forever.

Everyday Ulysses made a sacrifice to the Gods, begged for their intervention in his plight.

Chapter Twelve

New Year – New Enemies

11.45 PM
31st Dec 2015

Thea Spiteri had understood completely when, a few hours earlier, Helen Restin had said that she couldn't face the dawn of the New Year and had said that she just wanted to go to bed, sleep…..and hope that when she woke it had all been a dream: 'or should that be nightmare?' Spiteri watched as the desolate figure walked to her room, and gently closed the bedroom door behind her. Spiteri sat cross-legged on her living room floor, a glass of Merlot in one hand and a pen in the other. An A4 pad lay on the floor beside her with the not-too-inspired title of: '2016 – To Do'; emblazoned at the top. Spiteri had learned long ago that looking back only brought pain: *the future Thea, just think of the future.*

But, as she sat sipping her wine, waiting for the stroke of midnight to beckon in a New Year; she was totally unaware that the list she was compiling would bear no relation to the reality of what 2016 was about to bring.

*

Nicola Tizian had been compiling a 'To Do' List as well, but caution had taught him over the years that it was best to keep as little written down as possible. He preferred his lists to be in his head. He would have been happy had he known that Spiteri's list contained one item that was the same as one on his list: "Marriage." He would have been less happy to know that, on Spiteri's list, the word was followed by a question mark.

Although his bars and clubs were busy at this time of year; Tizian didn't enjoy the season. He would be glad once the third or fourth of January came around and all the stresses and strains of false bonhomie had passed for another year. He despised the fact that he had to give "presents" to politicians and local officials; and despised, even more, the Pulizija Officials who he knew would crucify him if they could, but were willing to leech from him while it was safe to do so. He knew his way of life was a huge burden for Thea Spiteri to carry and; if he was being honest, he too was beginning to find it a burden. *Marry Thea and take a step away from this life Nicola. Concentrate on the family; your own father showed it can be done.*

The arrival of Pietru Massa on Malta, and the revelations he had brought with him; had completely thrown Nicola Tizian, but there was only one more issue to deal with surrounding that, and then he was going to review his whole lifestyle. The previous night Tizian and Massa had gone for a Chinese meal. On the front of the menu was a little tag line saying that: "2016 was going to be the Year of the Monkey.....a very good thing." Tizian had taken heart from that: *Yes, 2016.....a very good thing.* If he had delved a little deeper, he would have discovered that 2016 was, in fact, the "Year of the Fire Monkey" and terrible results could come from bad decisions; and Nicola Tizian would have harder decisions to make than ever before.

*

Friday
1ˢᵗ Jan 2016
2.00 am
Thea Spiteri woke with a sore neck from where she had managed to fall asleep with her head against the armrest of her couch. After a few seconds, she gathered her thoughts and stretched away the stiffness creeping in as a result of sleeping on the floor. The A4 pad she had been working on, slipping off her knees. Spiteri picked it up and read over it.

2016 – To Do
Who would want Sarstedt dead?
Speak to Nicola about Sarstedt. See if he mentions Sarti. Could he be behind Sarstedt killing???? How can there be a connection with JFK?????
Find Red.
Marriage!!??

Right Thea, 'the living' come first; even the 'maybe' living, time to speak to '86' again.

Her house phone rang. 'A very Happy New Year, Thea.' *He's letting me know that he has my home number too.*
'What is it exactly that you want from me?'

'Did you research Watergate?'

'A bit.'

'So you will be aware of the role the mysterious "Deep Throat" played in the search for the truth?'

'Are you saying you will be my "Deep Throat".....is that what this is all about?'

'Exactly.'

'Then you'd better begin.'

'I already have; I have prepared three short lessons for you.'

'For God's sake.....OK, OK....these lessons are?'

'Thank you, Thea. Always remember, patience is a virtue as they say! Lesson 1 is simple: do not think of individuals. Lesson 2: friends can be enemies....and vice versa...'

'Oh, Christ.....look.....whoever you are.....'

'Do you want Lesson 3 or not?'

'Right....give it to me.'

'That's good.....because it's on your front door. Nice Christmas garlands you have Thea; good taste. Goodbye, I will call you soon.'

*

Two other women were sitting in their respective living rooms at the exact same time as Thea Spiteri; and having the same thought: *the living come first.*

But their thoughts on how to affirm that view were the polar opposite of Spiteri's.

*

Peter O'Toole never knew that it was a New Year. He was never sure if it was day or night; what the day was or the month. But one thing he did know; he knew that one day he would leave this place. Not the same man who came there perhaps, but he would leave nevertheless. A limousine would come for him. It would be so big that it would have a bath in it. He would wash and shave; put on fresh clothes. Instruct the driver to: 'Drop me at "Malachy's" young man.' He knew all this was true. He knew because Ithaca told him so.

Chapter Thirteen

Spiteri rushed to her front door. Her hands were sweating but she pulled the door open; half expecting nothing to be there and half in trepidation of what might be.

A large brown envelope sat incongruously against a plastic Santa that Spiteri had bought on a whim several years before and who, for some incomprehensible reason, had a fishing rod in his hand and appeared to be crying.

Spiteri looked around, saw nothing, lifted the envelope and retreated into her lounge; after double locking the front door.

A few moments later, Spiteri retrieved a single sheet of paper from the envelope.

Superintendent: as a Pulizija officer you will appreciate that hearsay is not fact or proof. Therefore, I am not going "tell" you things and expect you to just accept what I say. I want you to research everything and form your own conclusions.

Enclosed are several sheets of "facts"......verify or dismiss them. I will call you soon. There will be further envelopes and follow-up calls, but what you actually "do" with this information is up to you.

The purpose of this first envelope is to get you to ponder Lessons 1 & 2.

Dates & Places

1960
USA
17th March - The CIA ask President Eisenhower for approval to invade Cuba. He agrees.

18th Nov – President-Elect JF Kennedy is assured by CIA Head: Allen Dulles; that the plan will work. Kennedy is unconvinced but does not block the operation.

Dimona
Israel
President Eisenhower asks Israel what the
structure they are building at Dimona is. He is
told it is an agricultural plant.

1961
Washington DC
USA

20th Jan – JFK inaugurated as the 35th President of USA. He is the youngest ever President.
He is also the first Catholic to hold the post and
the first non-freemason since Lincoln.

February
Surveillance pics show that the plant at
Dimona, Israel; is for nuclear weapons development. Kennedy vehemently opposes the move.

17th April
USA / Cuba
An armed attack on Cuba, orchestrated by the
CIA and FBI, ends in disaster and humiliation for
President Kennedy. Kennedy immediately fires
the then head of the CIA: Allen Dulles; and lets it

be known that J Edgar Hoover's time as head of the FBI is also being re-evaluated.

Robert Kennedy is pressing on with hard-hitting anti-Mafia legislation; and both brothers are working on an initiative to end the strangle-hold that the Rothschild and Rockefellers dynasties hold on US and world economies; including disbanding the Federal Reserve Bank altogether.

1963
18th May
Washington
Kennedy's patience with Israel runs out and he informs Prime Minister Ben Gurion that if he does not allow US Inspectors into Dimona then he will ban all trade with Israel; including financial donations from the huge Jewish diaspora resident in the USA.

May / June
Marseilles
France

Christian David, the leader of the Corsican drug trafficking network in South America is in Marseilles, France to meet with the head of the Corsican Mafia: Antoine Guerini. At the meeting,

David is offered the contract to recruit a team to assassinate "the highest vegetable." David refused the contract as he thought attempting it in the USA was madness. The contract was however accepted by another Corsican drug dealer and killer named Lucien Sarti; and two other members of the Marseilles mob.

October
USA

John F Kennedy, President of the USA, is sitting in the White House Oval Office with his brother Robert. They are putting together the programme that they hope will propel Kennedy to a second term in office.

As well as his long-running plans; JFK is committed to resolving the Viet Nam situation. He had sent two aides to Viet Nam; the "McNamara-Taylor Mission to South Vietnam." He had now studied their findings and decided on a number of actions including:

The immediate withdrawal of 1,000 troops
'All out' by 1965

Many who profited in a variety of ways: political, economic, military....and ideologically [the Catholic and Jewish hierarchies were strong supporters of the war] were enraged by Kennedy's plans. JFK was unmoved and draughted the legislation.

<u>November</u>

10th – Lucien Sarti and two other men fly into Mexico City from France. All three men were travelling on Italian passports. From there they are driven to Brownsville, Texas. Once across the border they are picked up by an 'escort' supplied by Santo Trafficante, Jr of the New Orleans Mafia; a close ally of Antoine Guerini. They do not stay in a hotel but are kept in a safe house organised by Carlos Marcello, another New Orleans mobster.

22nd
Midday - Kennedy assassinated
1.30 pm – Lee Harvey Oswald arrested inside "The Texas Theatre" as he watches a movie.
3.30 pm - Flying to Washington in Air Force 1 – newly sworn in President Lyndon Johnson is informed that JFK had been assassinated by a "lone gunman."

Sat 23rd 8.30 am – CIA Director John McCone arrives at the White House. He is ushered inside and within a few minutes he has signed "National Security Memorandum 278; a classified document which immediately reversed Kennedy's decision to de-escalate the war in Viet Nam.

10.00 am - Future President George Bush Snr personally debriefed by J Edgar Hoover - "Lone Gunman" confirmed.

Mon 25th Nov – Under intense questioning from the media as to how the Lee Harvey Oswald "Lone Gunman" theory had been announced so quickly; Dallas D A Henry Wade blurts out: "we have his fingerprints on the gun."

29th - The Warren Commission is set-up to investigate the assassination. The Commission was to be headed by:...... Allen Dulles....the former head of the CIA.....sacked 2 years earlier by Kennedy.

<u>December</u>
Montreal
Canada

4th - A container ship: the "Velázquez", under commission to a company registered in Mexico City, leaves Montreal Harbour on a two-month trip. She is bound for a final destination of

Malta....where she is to unload various crates......with berthing in France, Corsica and Italy along the way.

Chapter Fourteen

Monday
4th Jan 2016
Spiteri's Office
Floriana

Spiteri had been frustrated that the holiday season had held up any investigative work being done on her outstanding cases, but the holidays were over now, and Mifsud and Said too were eager to get things moving again.

After three coffees were delivered, Spiteri wasted no more time: 'OK, we now know that we are looking at two murders; Stephen Muscat and Sarstedt…..and the two Restin deaths are still 'Open.' I'm sorry that I'm being vague about Sarstedt but it's out of my hands; although I am going to be questioning someone this afternoon. If I can tell you anything then, I will.

'Raul, I want you and Sarah to concentrate on the "Missing Men" list Sarah has drawn up. Why? Because years ago I worked on a case that was never solved, a man named Peter O'Toole aka 'Red' went missing. I've assumed that he is dead, but a mentally ill man who has seemed to appear from nowhere has been talking about "men, others, music, togas…..and someone called Red. We have to concentrate on that at the moment in case there is any chance that Red, or anyone else, is alive somewhere, and being held against their will.'

'When did Red go missing, Ma'am?' asked Raul.

Said answered: '1994': before Spiteri got the chance to reply. 'Obviously, our dead body, Stephen Muscat, is on the list after going missing in 2001.' Said then handed Spiteri and Mifsud a sheet of paper each. 'Will I carry-on, Ma'am?'

'Yes, please do Sarah.'

'I put in a date range of 1970 to 2015 be-cause, to be honest, I only expected about four names. I was wrong. Between 1970 and 1980 alone there were 5 men reported missing. Between 80 and 90.....11 reported missing. Between 90 and 2000....13 reported missing. Between 2000 and now; wait for it....51 men reported missing. Now some of this increase can be put down to better reporting procedures, and a lot of the people reported missing weren't Maltese.'

'What do you mean?' asked Mifsud.

'Well a couple were holiday makers, campers etc who may just have moved on, or even just gone home; probably never even knew they were reported missing. But the main reason is that a lot of the people are from Africa, Bangladesh, the Philippines.....they 'want' to disappear, if you get my meaning.'

'Yes, I think we do, Sarah. So, OK, let's concentrate on Maltese and European men. What are those numbers?'

'6 Europeans, including 2 British; and 10 Maltese males; but of those, only 6 are unaccounted for if you still count Stephen Muscat.'

'Names and stories?'

'OK, but can I just add one thing. Of the 10 who turned up; none of them were willing to speak to Pulizija, 3 subsequently committed suicide, 4 ended up in mental institutions and the other 3 left Malta for good.'

'Interesting' responded Spiteri.

'That's not all.'

'OK, go on.'

'All 10 were divorced within a year of turning up.'

'What do you think that tells us?' asked Mifsud.

'No idea, I'm only the messenger' replied Said with a slight smile.

'Good work Sarah. I've no idea what all this means either, but we're going to find out.'

*

That evening three women sat in their own homes and pondered the future. Two of the women; Miriam Zammit and Adrianne Valetta had red circles around the following Monday's date: 11th Jan 2016. Miriam Zammit had added "MG – Trial"; Adrianne Valletta had added "BASTARD!!"

Zammit knew that she had to hear this final case in a completely impartial and fair way; but, equally, she was determined that no 'outside interference' would be allowed to influence the procedures. Zammit knew that, on both counts, she would be struggling. *Michael Grech is as guilty as they come. The same man does not get accused of rape four times, by four different women; although only two went as far as a trial, as well as lesser assaults, without being a monster. My final act will be to nail you, Grech; friends in high places or not.*

Adrianne Valetta too wanted justice, not just for herself but for all female victims of Grech and *the other monsters* walking about Malta in cloaks of respectability. Both women also knew that one way or another, Grech would pay this time.

*

Spiteri's musings were interrupted by her phone ringing.

'Good evening, Thea. I hope you have had time to look over the dates I gave you; and to verify the ones that you could. It is very important that I let you know who the players; or should that be forces; that are at play here are….and for me to gain your trust. So, to do that, I gave you some facts and dates.'

Spiteri looked at her phone in the vain hope that it would reveal something, anything, about the caller.

'Listen….'Deep Throat'….or whoever you are. Just tell me what it is that you want to tell me. I can assure you that if you keep up these nuisance calls I will eventually trace you, so tell me now then go to hell.'

'Thea, I told you; I cannot just 'tell you' as that would just be hear-say. I will point you in the right direction; you must search for the truth, and when you find it you will know it to be true.'

The voice continued: 'Keep that sheet of dates as a template. I'll fill in gaps along the way.

In Nov of 1960, the 15th to be exact, the then Boss of the Chicago Mafia; Sam Giancana "fixes" the <u>1960 U.S. presidential election</u>-day results in <u>Cook County, Illinois</u>, in favour of <u>Sen.</u> <u>John F. Kennedy</u>, of Massachusetts. In 1961, the new President appoints his brother, <u>Robert Kennedy</u>, as <u>U.S. Attorney General</u>. Robert Kennedy would be hailed as: ".......the first attorney general of the United States to make a serious attack on the Mafia and organised crime."

On Nov 30th 1961 – President-Elect John F. Kennedy allows "<u>Operation Mongoose</u>," a plan to assassinate the Cuban leader <u>Fidel Castro</u>; to go ahead after getting assurances on the outcome from the CIA and FBI. In cooperation with the CIA, the federal government is planning to use contacts like Sam Giancana and the Boss of South Florida, Santos Trafficante; who practically ran Havana before the revolution, to carry out this operation. The plan failed. A top-ranking CIA official; namely Allen Dulles, was fired from the CIA for the failure. Take a note of that name please, Thea.'

'So you are saying that the Mafia killed Kennedy, and the CIA covered it up? Hardly original, Mr....'

'Please just call me Hunter....not Mr Hunter.....just Hunter. You will understand the irony in time. In answer to your question; no, I am absolutely not saying that. This investigation is not about individual people; it's not even about one or two Groups, it is about a cabal, an unholy alliance of darkness. Like I said, I am merely setting the stage at this point.'

'OK, go on.'

'No, I will go now. I would like you to check the facts I have just given you. I need you to be happy that I'm telling you the truth in these matters. You need to have fully grasped the basics before we can go onto more serious matters.'

'More serious!...... than the assassination of a President? You surprise me. Your two countrymen feel nothing is more important than that.'

'Ah, you think I am American? How interesting. One thing the next few weeks will show you Thea; no-one is who they appear to be. In fact, I will set you a task: research all you can about a man called E. Howard Hunt.

Goodbye, Thea.....I will call soon.'

*

Tuesday
5th Jan 2016
Thea Spiteri had heard from the Care Home
that 86 seemed to be at his most lucid first thing
in the morning; and so she found herself standing
at the side of his bed at 7.00 am with a coffee, 4
filled baguettes and four doughnuts. The coffee
was for her; the food for the 'perpetually rav-
enous' 86.

'Good Morning, 86…..I've brought you
some breakfast. Is it OK for me to come over
and give you it.'

'Are there maggots in it?'

'No!'

'Oh, I like maggots.'

Spiteri decided to try and differentiate between 86's havering and any reality that may hit
him from time to time.

'Is it OK if I have one of the doughnuts, 86?'

'No.'

'OK. Is it OK if I talk to you while you're
having your food?'

86 pointed to a young nurse who was bend-
ing over a bedside cabinet at the far end of the
room.

'She wants my cock.'

Spiteri knew she was floundering already: 'Oh, what makes you think that?'

'They all want it.'

'Whose "they"?'

'Girls.'

'Right. Were there any girls with you when you were away?'

86 seemed to physically drift away: 'Away?'

'Yes, you've been away. But you're back now; you're safe.'

'Safe.'

'Can you remember your name? Not your '86' name…..your name when you were safe before?'

'Safe?'

'Yes.'

'Stephen.'

'Stephen…..your name was Stephen?'

'No.'

'Who is Stephen?'

'Stephen's away.'

'Is Red away?'

'No!! Red is in the kitchen.'

'What is he doing in the kitchen?'

'Talking to Ithaca you stupid bitch!!'

'Of course, sorry. Who is Ithaca?'

'His friend.'

'Is Ithaca a man or a woman?'

'John is a man. Oh yes, John is a man.'

'John? Is John in the kitchen too?'

'Noooo!! John is in the bar. You fucking whore.'

'I think you should leave it there, Superintendent. Don't worry, it's not you, his mood swings are the stuff of legend' said the Head Care Home Nurse.

'OK, thank you, I will. Just one last question: '86, before you were safe....were you tied up?'

Two baguettes and two doughnuts slid onto the floor as 86 pulled the bed covers over his head, and curled up under them. He never spoke.

Before leaving, Spiteri walked down the hallway with the Head Nurse: 'What age would you say he is?'

'So difficult to say really. I imagine that whatever horrors he's been through would put forty years on anyone's looks.'

'I've got to find out where he's been all this time. I think other lives may depend on that.'

Spiteri pulled her mobile out of her bag on the way back to her car.

'Sarah, the six men still missing; get everything you can on them I'll meet you and Raul in my office at 1.00 pm.'

Spiteri didn't wait for a reply before phoning Tizian.

'Nicola, where are you?'

'In your heart, I hope.'

'Nicola, I'm not in the mood. Where are you, we need to talk.'

'I can be at my office in half an hour if you want?'

'I want.' Spiteri again hung up without waiting for a response.

When Spiteri arrived at Nicola Tizian's office, he was already there.

'Thea, you sounded stressed; is everything OK?'

'If you wanted to keep a man, two men….six men…...captive for years, decades….where would you keep them?'

A smile started to form on Tizian's lips, but he could tell that Spiteri was serious.

'Captive….for decades…...I have no idea. Why are you asking such a question?'

'Because I think someone on this island is doing just that. The problem is I have no idea where to start looking.'

Spiteri saw Tizian's eyes narrow: 'Nicola, what is it?'

'Over the years, I've heard stories about men going missing; but they have mostly turned up. One of them worked for me at one time. Sad tale.'

'Tell me.'

'Nothing to tell really. He went missing one day……turned up 2 or 3 days later…..but, let's just say he wasn't the same man when he returned. He went mad eventually….killed himself.'

'What do you mean by "not the same man"?'

'His private parts had been violated; a knife, a razor….who knows.'

'Why wasn't this reported to the Pulizija?'

'Ha….are you serious? What real man is going to announce to the world that he is no longer a man?'

'Macho fucking bullshit, Nicola. It could have stopped it happening again…..and again.'

Tizian made no reply.

'The body in the Blue Lagoon; Sarstedt.'

'What about him?'

'Did you know him?'

'I can't recall.'

'That's odd; you owned a business with him.'

Spiteri saw a furrow appear on Tizian's brow. He paused……

'Ah yes, I remember now…..but no, I never did go into business with him. A mutual friend put us together for a possible importing business, but nothing came of it. I did some research on him; let's just say he had enemies that I didn't wish to be my enemies. I never actually met him, though.'

Spiteri wasn't satisfied but knew there was no point in pursuing things, and Tizian's story did fit in with the little the Commissioner had told her. As she rose to leave, she opted for some small talk: 'When are you going to introduce me to your friend?'

Tizian looked puzzled: 'My friend?'

'Yes, your old boyhood friend; I believe he's staying with you for a while.'

'Are you checking up on me, Thea?'

'No, I took you up on your offer to drop in to see you. I came the other day, but you were already in full voice.'

'For goodness sake, you should have said; come and joined us. Yes, Tony is staying with me for a few days. He's going back to the USA soon, though.'

'OK, I'll call you.'

*

Mists of Time

Zeus, God of Gods, loved his wife; Athena. Her advice was always sound. "Enough time has passed....tell Calypso to release Ulysses....let him go home to his wife."

Calypso could not defy a Deity. She provided a boat and supplies and ordered the winds to carry 'her love' home. Any other man who sought refuge on her island would pay for her torment.

Chapter Fifteen

Ithaca scampered away when the door opened. The man once known as Red looked up from his prone and shackled position in the corner.

"My beautiful lover; you are the only one who has stayed at my side. I will reward you. The apparition floated towards her lover; ran her fingers through his tangled, filthy hair. She gently ran her fingernails over his bloodied cheeks; down over his naked body....down, down they went....her fingers expertly parted the greying mass of pubic hair....

Peter O'Toole knew that his screams would not be heard, his pleas would go unanswered......but he screamed anyway.

*

Mifsud and Said were sitting outside Spiteri's office as she dashed along the corridor at 1.15 pm: 'I'm so sorry, I got held up with this Sarstedt thing.'

'Any progress?' asked Mifsud.

'Not really. Right; Missing Men...Sarah?'

'Yes, as I said 6 men were never accounted for. The first one was a Josef Calleja who went missing in 1973.'

'Where from?'

'Sliema.'

'Who reported it?'

'His wife.'

'Age?'

'40.'

'OK, so he would be, what, 83 years old now. So, 86 isn't him. Next one?'

'Martin Camilleri. Missing since 1980. Twenty years old then. Reported missing from Gharb, on Gozo, by his mother. He would be 56 if he's still alive.'

'A possible for "86" but I don't think so. Next?'

'John Rizzo. Missing since 1987. He was 25, so he would be 54 today. Went missing from Mosta; reported missing by his boss at a cleaning agency.'

'Again; possibly, but......OK, next.'

'Peter O'Toole aka Red: Missing from Marsascala, 1994. No known family here. Age not known, but thought to be in his early 40's.'

'This was the one I worked on for a while. He could be alive, but he's not "86"....I would have recognised him. Next.'

'Stephen Muscat. Reported missing by his wife in 2001. We now know he was murdered, or at least, died, about 8 years ago.'

'What did the PM show?'

'Well, he had definitely been tortured but she couldn't say for sure how he died.'

'Right, well he's definitely not "86"....last one?'

'Ramon Pace: Went missing on his lunch break from work in the Sweigi area in 2008. He was 30 years old and a Pension Fund Manager. Single, "bit weird" according to some of his fellow workers, the women especially didn't like him apparently. No family; reported missing by his boss.'

'Could be him. Right, Raul, get over to the Care Home, take a pic of "86" on your phone; go to his old company, there must be people still there who will remember him. Sarah, get a hold 2 or 3 of the longest serving officers you can; but ones who are still in uniform, the more 'ear to the ground' ones. Get them into a room, coffee and cakes, get them to discuss "from their much-admired knowledge of the islands" where they think men could be held captive for decades.'

Spiteri's phone rang: 'Yes, Commissioner.'

'Are you close to my office, Superintendent?'

'Yes, I'm…..'

'Come over straight away then please.'

'Yes, Commissioner, thank you Commissioner…..civility costs nothing, Commissioner' said Spiteri to the dead line.

*

Adrianne Valletta wiped the blood from her hands and soaked the flowing white beach dress she so loved in cold water and bleach. *That was careless Adrianne, you stupid girl.* She knew the looming court case was distracting her and she had finally managed to "let go" some of her demons; but she had to stay focused, had to get Michael Grech to pay: *simply have to.*

*

Similar to her last visit, Thea Spiteri was ushered straight into the Commissioner's Office by his secretary. As she had expected; Carter and

Clark had returned from the USA and were looking for a progress report on the Sarstedt / Sarti killing. The Commissioner motioned for Spiteri to take a seat just as his desk intercom buzzed: 'Yes.'

'Mr Grech is on the phone Commissioner; he says it's urgent.'

'It always is with him. Tell him I'm tied up for the next hour, he can call back then…..and no more calls please.'

'Yes; Commissioner.'

'So, Superintendent, any progress with this Sarti case?'

'No.'

'No….that's it….no?' said Carter.

'Well, I can lie if you like, but the reality is that we haven't made any progress…and, if you don't mind me saying, you people have been working on this case for 50 years and turned up one suspect; and couldn't even keep him safe for 1 day.'

'Did you talk to your; eh……friend?'

'If by that you mean my, eh…..partner, then yes, I did. He admitted that many years ago he had considered a business proposition that involved Sarstedt, but it never got off the ground, and he never actually met him.'

'Did he say anything about who he thought would want Sarti dead?'

'Yes.'

'Who?'

'Half the population of USA, by the sounds of it. He had many enemies by all accounts.'

'You don't seem very cooperative Superintendent; if you don't mind me saying so.'

'You know what, you people make me laugh. You come here, steal our Ballistics Report, steal the bullet involved in a killing here, refer with obvious disdain to my "friend".....and then want to know why I haven't solved in a week or so, a case you've been working on for 50 years. Let me tell you something guys, I've got one, possibly three other murders to work on; I'm searching for a missing person who may just still be alive after 22 years of captivity, and my faith in anything you say is fucking nil. If and when I know anything that I think you should know, I'll be in touch.'

Spiteri rose and headed for the door: 'Oh my "friend" did say two things you might be interested in.'

'What were they?'

'One: it's common knowledge that it wasn't Oswald who shot your President.' Spiteri moved half-way through the door: Clark shouted 'and the second thing?'

'Oh yeah, the CIA were involved. Bye for now.'

Commissioner Malia had taken up his usual position of staring out of the window; only this time he was smiling.

Thea Spiteri was still spitting fire when she got to her car: *who the fuck do these people think they are? A couple of bottles of wine; and an evening in with Helen, now the order of the day, Thea.*

Thea Spiteri would indeed enjoy her evening, and a phone call she would receive the following morning would lift her spirits even further; but the response to one she herself makes will lead eventually to total despair.

Chapter Sixteen

Weds morning

Thea Spiteri had enjoyed her evening with Helen Restin. They had relaxed and reminisced about their lives, and Spiteri had marvelled at how calm and philosophical Helen Restin appeared to be about the double tragedy that had engulfed her.

Restin was still asleep in bed at 8.00am but Spiteri was up and just about ready to leave for work when her mobile rang: 'Yes, Raul.'

'Sorry to call so early Ma'am, but I thought you'd want to know; 86 is definitely Ramon Pace.

I couldn't track anyone from his old office down yesterday, but I got the address of his former boss; the guy who reported him missing, he's confirmed it's Pace.'

'Excellent; well done. I'll call you later.'

Spiteri searched in her pocket for her car keys, and along with the keys pulled out a crunched-up piece of paper: "Pietru Massa?": written in her own hand. She was at a loss at first as to why she had written the name down, but then realised it was the name of Nicola's 'friend'. She left the house and walked to her car. As she got ready to start the engine, a nagging thought came into her head. *Pietru? That's not the name Nicola gave me; I'm sure it isn't….but why would he lie about something like that?* Spiteri sat and pondered for a few more minutes: *you must do it, Thea….for your own sanity if nothing else.* She picked up her mobile and dialled.

'Carter.'

'Yes, hello, it's Superintendent Spiteri. Look I'm just calling to apologise about my comments yesterday but I have a lot on, and not much to go on from your end. Anyway, I'm sorry.'

'That's OK, Super…..I like feisty, shows you have passion.'

Spiteri rolled her eyes: *he even sounds like a TV cop.* 'So, listen, a name has come up, it's probably nothing; not connected at all, but could you run a check on a US citizen for me. Nothing deep; just an overview.'

'Sure; is the guy connected to Sarstedt in some way?'

'No, no….it's another case entirely but I just thought, you know, an American…..best to be thorough.'

'Sure thing; and you'll let us know straight away if our case is affected?'

'Sure thing partner' Spiteri had to conceal her laughter.

'What's the name?'

'Pietru Massa.'

'Thank you, Ma'am'

Spiteri hung up feeling slightly guilty on two counts: checking up on Nicola, and parodying a fellow officer. *Not nice, Thea…..he is a fellow law enforcement officer after all.*

Spiteri started her car and set-off: giving a 'He-Ha cowboy' screech through her sunroof as she left her driveway.

*

Wednesday Evening…….

Michael Grech picked up the telephone receiver in the Guard Office, and dismissed the guard with a wave of the hand. The guard said nothing.

'George, I know you are a busy man, so I won't keep you long' he said, with no introductory formalities. 'I expect to be out of this terrible place no later than next Wednesday. Do you understand that George?'

'It's not that simple, Michael. It has to be done in such a way that no probing questions are asked.'

'On the contrary George; it is very simple. Get me out of here, or you will be joining me.'

'You're not as powerful as you think you are, Grech.'

'Perhaps, but what is it they say; the camera never lies? I'm assuming that includes videos of grown men frolicking naked with young boys. What do you think, George?'

'Fuck you, Grech.'

'George, get me out of here…..and I'll gladly grant your request. It was a request I take it, George…..and not a threat?'

The line went dead.

'You may man your office again Mr Guard' said, Grech, as he strolled, hands in pockets, along the corridor to his cell.

*

Red O'Toole was angry with Ithaca. He hadn't visited him that day, and hadn't left a note. *That is fine by me my friend. When you come tomorrow it will be my turn to completely ignore you. And I shall…..oh yes I shall alright.*

*

Adriane Valetta packed the scraps of food into her bag. This was the part of her day she hated the most. She hated it even more than the hosing away of the shit and blood. She hated it because when they got the food they were grateful, saw her as a friend: *Well, I am not your friend, disgusting animals, every one of you; and when your time comes you will die.*

*

Helen Restin had never felt at ease answering the house phone in Thea Spiteri's house, but her friend had assured her that it was fine; if it was Pulizija business they would call her mobile, and even if they did phone her house for some reason, they would only speak to her: "so it's no problem at all, Helen."

She picked up on the second ring. It was a Jack Carter looking for Thea. Helen explained that Spiteri was out at the moment. 'Oh that's OK, I just had a little bit of info on that Massa guy she asked me to check out…..I'll give her a call back in the morning.'

Chapter Seventeen

When the Spiteri's phone rang the next morning, Carter was keeping his word. She prayed it was some form of good news.

'Ma'am, it's Jack Carter.'

'Good morning, Jack. How are you?'

'I'm dandy. I'm just calling to say that we did that name check for you; the guy Massa?'

'Oh yes; good……and….'

'Oh, he's clean, no record of any kind.'

'OK, thank you' Spiteri exhaled rather than said: 'that's a big help. Can you email me his pic anyway?'

'That's OK Ma'am, glad to help. Yea, sure......bit of guy too by all accounts.'

'Oh, why's that?'

'Successful. You know how we Americans love a success story; The American Dream....and stuff like that.'

'Good for him. Thanks, Jack.'

'Anytime, Super.'

*

Mifsud and Said were sitting beside the bed of the man formerly known as "86". Only on this occasion the stakes were much higher. 10 euro higher to be precise; the amount Said and Mifsud had bet each other as to who would break through to Raymond Pace first.

'Hello, Ramon, how are you today?' asked Said.

'Wet.'

'Wet! No, you're not wet Ramon; you are nice and comfortable in your clean bed.'

'No! Wet! I'm always wet on a Friday!'

'Ramon; is it Friday today?' interrupted Mifsud.

'Yes.'

Mifsud turned to Said: 'I think I'm getting through.'

'How do you know it's Friday today Ramon? Did someone tell you it was Friday?'

'No.'

'Then how do you know?'

'Because I'm wet!'

'What's making you wet Ramon, is it the rain?' said Said.

'Stephen's gone…..but Red is still in the kitchen.'

'What's making you wet Ramon, are you in a bath?'

'Bath? No baths.'

'A shower then; do you like showers?'

'The water is cold…..oh yes, very cold.'

'Where did Stephen go, Ramon?' asked Mifsud.

'It's a secret…..ssshhhh.'

'Won't you just tell me the secret, Ramon? I have food here for you if you do.'

'Food?'

'Yes.'

'With maggots?'

'No, no maggots today; but it is lovely food….and I have a beer for you.'

'Give me it.'

'I will, Ramon…..but first, you have to tell me about Stephen.'

'Stephen? OK; but not you….her.'

Said smiled over at Mifsud with an air of satisfaction: 'Get the 10 euros out sucker' Said
smirked at a crestfallen Mifsud.

'Come close….it's a secret.'

Said bent and leant over Ramon Pace.

'Is your fanny wet?……hahahahaha……Red's
in the kitchen!'

*

Pulizija Constable Nichols was a happy man.
He had just finished his shift and was on the ferry
to Gozo with his wife of over thirty years. They
would spend the weekend going for walks,
drinking wine, talking about nothing in particular….and watching the sunsets over Ramla Bay,
from the porch of the wooden "Summer House"
his father had built from broken pallets, drift-
wood, discarded window frames and local
sandstone bricks decades before. Constable
Nichols and his wife thought it was the nicest
place on earth. It allowed people the space to
think, and Constable Nichol's thoughts were
about to change a number of lives forever.

Chapter Eighteen

"I'm forty three years old; I'm not going to die in office. So the vice presidency doesn't mean anything."

{JFK, to his aide Kenneth O'Donnell; on being forced to take Lyndon B. Johnson as his VP: July 11, 1963.}

***

Monday 11th Jan 2016

'Good morning, Thea.' Spiteri recognised Hunter's voice now.

'Good morning.'

'Well, are you satisfied by what I have told you so far?'

'As satisfied as one can be in these circumstances.'

'What do you mean?'

'The information you have given me appears sound, but so does other information that I've seen on the Internet.'

'That will change Thea....believe me.'

'So.....have you more to tell me today?'

'Yes, but you have to go somewhere first.....I can't always hand deliver!'

'OK, where?'

'Be at Villa Blye in Paola at 11.00 am sharp tomorrow morning. Sit in your car. You will see a small boy coming and sitting on the villa steps. He will be carrying an envelope. Go over and ask him how to get to Mexico. He will hand you the envelope.'

'Mexico?'

'Why not?'

'Why not indeed?' sighed Spiteri.

*

Michael Grech swanned into the dock of the Court of Magistrates in Valetta as if he was on a stroll around a museum.

He briefly noticed Adrianne Valetta sitting in the Witness Room as he had ambled past but did not acknowledge her in any way. *I don't know her after all!*

Magistrate Zammit despised the man as he preened himself in the dock, but was resolute in her resolve that she would deal with this last case with complete impartiality. *But once you are found guilty my friend, then I will knock that smirk off your face.*

Adrianne Valetta had been saved the trauma of seeing Grech as he passed, but perhaps Grech would not have been so nonchalant had he properly seen the look of contentment on her face.

None of the three were aware that The Chief Justice Emeritus was sitting in the next room, monitoring the trial via the security cameras.

*

Sarah Said and Raul Mifsud were sitting in the Homicide Room discussing ways that they might be able to get through to 86, Ramon Pace.

There was a knock on the door and an elderly Constable came in, Said vaguely recognised him but was unsure where from. Mifsud merely nodded and looked away: *probably looking for donations for something.*

Constable Nichols walked over to Said's desk: 'Sargant, I was one of the officers at your meeting......the one about places on the islands where people may be held captive....Constable Nichols?'

'Oh, yes, of course.....please take a seat. Have you had an idea; I certainly hope so, because I haven't.'

'I have but I'm not, you know, saying that it's any good.....or that I have any proof to substantiate it.' Said smiled as she surmised that the second part had been hastily put in; in case he himself was suspected of something!

'Of course not.....please go on.....anything is worth considering.'

'Well, as I said; I was thinking......but first of all, can I see the list of the Missing Men please?'

'Of course' said Said as she dug a copy out from the mound of paper on her desk.'

'Mm.....Sergeant have you read Homer's Odyssey?'

'At school perhaps; why?'

'Let me tell you a shortened version. On his way back from victory at Troy, Odysseus was shipwrecked on the rocks off an island called, at that time, Ogygia. He was saved by the sea nymph, Calypso. Calypso then fell in love with Odysseus, or Ulysses if you prefer. Calypso was then associated for ever more with seduction and concealment. But Odysseus didn't want to stay with Calypso as he loved his wife, Penelope; and longed to be set free. After seven years, Zeus ordered Calypso to let him go.'

'An interesting story Constable but.......'

'Sergeant, the island of myth known as Ogygia......many believe it to be Malta.'

'Well that's as maybe....'

Nichols handed the list back to Said: 'look at the years.'

Said only needed a few seconds: 'Jesus..........every seven years.'

'It would seem you have a modern day Calypso on your hands, Sergeant.'

'Do you have any idea where these men may have been held?'

'Not at the moment; but I am thinking ...... and also going to the library to read over Homer's works. I will get back to you if I come up with anything.'

*

Miriam Zammit was frustrated and angry. She felt that she had spent the whole morning slapping down arguments from Michael Grech's lawyers that "there was no case to answer." Originally she had been pleased when she read in the citations who the Defense Lawyers would be: *they couldn't get a client off even if he was pardoned.* Now they were getting on her nerves by citing lack of forensic evidence, the alleged victim's hazy recollection of the evening, the defendants impeccable reputation and the "victim's well known promiscuous lifestyle." Zammit dismissed all the points with a contemptuous wave: 'Gentlemen, this trial will go ahead. Be ready to start tomorrow morning and no further delays. Understood?'

*

I don't know why you're shaking your head Ithaca. Guinness is the nectar of the Gods; the life blood of sanity; the water of life. When I get out of here I'll prove it to you. You can sit on the bar in Malachy's, your own bowl of the 'Dark Stuff' there in front of you……then we'll see who's right! Many a night I left there with too much blood in my alcohol! Ha! I'm not mad you know my friend; I'm not. Some who've been here went mad, some died I think, but not Red. No, not me; I'll walk out of here….and The Priestess of Pain will not stop me.

*

Michael Grech strode out of the court. He was slightly peeved that the case was going ahead but guessed that George wanted to put on the pretence of a show. Grech smiled: *freedom soon, Michael….freedom soon.*

Adrianne Valletta also strode out of the court. She had hoped not to give evidence but knew it was inevitable that she would have to; as Grech's vanity would never allow him to admit that he had to force his attentions on a woman. She too allowed herself a smile: *justice soon, Michael….justice soon.*

The Chief Justice Emeritus did not stride anywhere. He clasped his fingers on the desk in front of him: *finish this.*

*

Tuesday 12th
Midnight
Spiteri's Home

Thea Spiteri had been studying Hunter's latest pages; along with researching on the Internet, for 2 hours. For the first time, she actually wished Hunter would call. Her 'discoveries' were bothering her more and more. She scanned Hunter's sheets once more; then she studied again the disturbing notes she herself had made.

*

<u>1963</u>

I have listed a chain of events that all occurred in 1963. They are all verifiable.

In February of 1963, in a pizza parlour in Chicago, three Mafia Lieutenants are seated with a

French national; Antoine Guerini. He was a top ranking member of the notorious 'French Connection' cartel. The three mobsters were acting on behalf of Sam Giancana, Santos Trafficante and Carlos Marcello. The contract to recruit the hit-men to kill Kennedy apparently came from Trafficante as he had close European ties. However, and this is important Thea; Trafficante's lawyer; Frank Ragano, would admit years later that his client was indeed involved; but the order for the hit had come from "elsewhere." Again; that point is important, Thea. Remember it.

In March 1963 a Mr A. Hidell purchased, by mail order, a 6.5mm Carcano Model 91/38 carbine and a magnifier x 4 scope. The weapon was subsequently delivered to a different address, by persons unknown; and signed for in the name of Lee Harvey Oswald. This is the gun that will eventually be found by CIA and FBI agents on the floor of the Texas Book Depository.'

In May or June of '63; Guerini approached three Corsican hit men and offered them the contract on Kennedy. One of these men was Lucien Sarti, one of the other two was rumoured to be called Basti but the third name was never discovered. They accepted.

This next bit of information may appear un-important, but it is very important....as you will find out in due course.

In September 1963; Lee Harvey Oswald visit-ed Mexico City.

Thea – you will remember from the "Dates Sheet" that a Commission, the Warren Commis-sion, was set up in late Nov 1963 to look into the Kennedy assassination. The individual members of that Commission are listed below. Study them....and classify them...... in 'Groups.'

Warren Committee
- Earl Warren, Chief Justice of the United States (chairman) (1891–1974)
- Richard Russell, Jr. (D-Georgia), U.S. Senator, (1897–1971)
- John Sherman Cooper (R-Kentucky), U.S. Senator (1901–1991)
- Hale Boggs (D-Louisiana), U.S. Repre-sentative, House Majority Whip (1914–1972)
- Gerald Ford (R-Michigan), U.S. Repre-sentative (later 38th President of the United States), House Minority Leader (1913-2006)

Paul Vincent Lee

- Allen Welsh Dulles, former Director of Central Intelligence and head of the Central Intelligence Agency (1893–1969)
  - John J. McCloy, former President of the World Bank (1895–1989)

Earl Warren did not want to Chair the Commission as he knew it would be subject to political pressures. New President, Lyndon Johnson played a card that forced Warren to accept.

Allen Dulles, a man that had been sacked by Kennedy for lying about CIA operations, was on the Committee. Why?

John J McCloy, an international banker with close ties to the Federal Reserve Bank that Kennedy wanted to disband, was on the Committee. Why?

Gerald Ford, despite being found guilty of tampering with evidence to be presented to the Committee; eventually became President [Unelected]

Head of Administration to the Committee was George Bush Snr. He too would later become President, as would his son; George W Bush. His other son, Jeb Bush, although playing no 'active' role in the Commission, would influence it nevertheless. Part of Bush Snr's role; along with his team, was to 'filter' the evidence that was to be put before the Committee. His second-in-command in that team was; J Edgar Hoover….another Kennedy hater.

Examples of that 'filtering' are:

More than a hundred witnesses near the grassy knoll who heard a bang, then a pause, then a bang, bang, in a rapid-fire sequence not possible with a bolt action rifle. There was synchronisation, three salvos or volleys, as many as nine total shots fired. One hit the street, three hit JFK, two hit John Connolly, one nicked James Tague, one hit near a manhole cover and one hit a highway sign. All those shots can be accounted for, but, of course, the Warren Commission stuck with the story of only three shots were fired along with their cockamamie magic bullet theory which stated that one bullet caused seven wounds to two men, including a strike on bone, yet emerged unscathed and was found on a hospital stretcher later.

16 of these 'Grassy Knoll' witnesses were Secret Service personnel. 12 said the shots came from there. This was 'reported' by the Warren Committee as: "4 Secret Service personnel on the

Grassy Knoll said the shots didn't come from there."

In the Report, Oswald's motive was stated as "publicity-seeking" as, on his arrest, he said: "Now everyone will know who I am." But people present at the time stated that this line was said in fearful tones; not boastful ones.

NB Re No 1 above the 'card' played by LBJ was simple. Warren was the Grand Master Freemason of California and had to support his fellow Masons. Groups Thea, groups?

Chapter Nineteen

Weds 13th

The following morning Thea Spiteri was depressed more than angry. Her research into the murky waters of US politics was leaving her with more doubts about terms like "democracy" and "free world" than she would have thought possible. *If only a fraction of this information is true, then our world is run by banks, secret societies and the vested interests of suppliers to the military.*

As if on cue, Spiteri's mobile rang. She 'knew' it was Hunter.

'Good morning, Thea. I hope you slept well.'

'I'm not sure it's possible to sleep with all this stuff swirling about in my head. Not counting the murder and abduction investigations I also have to manage.

'Murders....plural?'

'Yes, three in all; a shooting and two 'some-things' out at the airport.'

'I have some connections with airport security, would you like me to ask.....off the record?'

'You can ask, but there isn't anything to find out I'm sure.'

'OK. Anyway;...........to work. Are you starting to see how the world works?'

'I'm assuming that your rather large hint about Freemasons was where you wanted me to go?'

'And.......?'

'Well it didn't take me too long to find that LBJ, Dulles, Hoover and Bush were, or are, all Freemasons; and Warren obviously.'

'And many others, but we will get to them. Did you manage to spot something on the flip side of that coin?'

'JFK was the first Catholic President; and the first non-Mason since Lincoln.'

'Correct. Let's move on. Did you look up Hunt?'

'Only a very basic look. He was CIA wasn't he?'

'Ha, amongst many things. I hope you are sitting comfortably, Thea. There is so much to say about Hunt that we would be talking for a year; fortunately, you just need the facts. Mr Hunt was ex-FBI, then CIA. He was an arranger of assassinations, for example, the failed attempt on Castro;......... Code Name: ZR/Rifle in case you want to check.

He was successful with many others, however. He also arranged Coup d'états. Again I will use the Cuban disaster as an example, for the simple reason that although JFK blamed Allen Dulles for the disaster; Hunt blamed JFK.....and never forgave him. Hunt was a long term friend of Lyndon Johnson, and ended up a Plumber for Tricky Dickie Nixon.'

'Sorry....did you just say he was a plumber?'

'Ha, glad to see you are actually listening, Thea.'

'In this case, "plumber" was the name given to "special" agents.....ones who "fixed leaks." '

'Very droll.'

'So, when Nixon got himself too involved in things he shouldn't have; guns for drugs being an example, his political opponents smelt blood. So he ordered a break-in at their headquarters. Oh, I nearly forgot, remember I told you that it was important to make a note of Mexico?'

'Yes.'

'…and that Lee Harvey Oswald spent some time there not long before the killing.'

'So?'

'Well guess who was running CIA operations in Mexico at that time?'

'I'm guessing Hunt.'

'Correct again. So, back to Watergate. The Democratic Party Headquarters were situated in the now infamous Watergate Building. They got caught, Nixon was forced to resign, and Gerard Ford became unelected President. It was Hunt and his brother who "managed" the break-in. When more came to light over the years about Hunt's dirty deeds, a paper published an article linking him to the JFK assassination. He sued, and won $650,000. The paper appealed, and won their case.

Later, Hunt was once again in court when another paper printed a grainy picture of four vagrants who were arrested in Dealey Plaza on the day of the shooting. The paper claimed that one of the men was Hunt. He sued, claiming he was in Washington DC that day. The paper proved he wasn't. He said he had been mixed up and meant to say he was shopping in Chinatown. An investigation was mounted and found that the store Hunt claimed to be in didn't exist. Hunt dropped the case.'

'But hold on. If all you are saying is true; why wasn't he charged?'

'Thea, can't you see it yet? Everyone involved is in a tight group, and they all protect each other. Do you honestly think that people in, or formerly in, the CIA are going to admit that the thing is rotten to the core?' After the Bay of Pigs, JFK promised to "splinter the CIA into a thousand pieces and scatter it to the winds." He may as well have written his own death warrant.'

'OK, but it's still only conjecture isn't it?'

'No. Just before he died, Hunt brought out a book. He left some passages out because he didn't want to face perjury charges over previous statements given under oath. His sons published them after his death. Hunt named himself and LB Johnson; and Meyer, Harvey, Morales [three former CIA operatives]....and the shooter; "The Frenchman on the Grassy Knoll"........ Lucien Sarti.'

'Fuck.'

'I'm nearly done; but not quite. Thea, find out the following: who Alpha 66 were……..and the name of the man who shot Oswald.'

'I thought it was Jack Ruby!'

'His real name! Finally, find out now who it was that managed to get Oswald; an unemployed weirdo with no qualifications, a job in the Texas Book depository, a week after Johnson had managed to get Kennedy's itinerary changed to include Dallas.'

'But none of this tells me why getting this gun now is so important. Besides, according to you, there were 3 shooters; that means three guns.'

'Correct again. Two of the guns were left behind by the shooters.'

'So what happened to them?'

'They got "lost." '

'You're not serious?'

'I wish I wasn't. Thea, you are a murder investigator, treat the Kennedy killing as your own case. Solve it and you will know.'

'Wait a minute. All this stuff you're giving me is fascinating in a way, but you haven't really told me anything that Carter and Clark haven't. They told me from the beginning that Oswald was innocent.   I'm not getting just why you are telling me this stuff.'

'Thea, everything I tell you is true; some of what our two CIA friends are telling you is true, but not it all.'

'Give me an example, something I can use in the future if I have to confront them.'

'Well, Lucien Sarti did not die in a brothel in France; I can tell you that.'

Spiteri was stunned: 'How did you know they told me that?'

'Because they would not be here if they weren't the type to follow the party line.'

'Even so, the truth is that the CIA and Freemasonry……and JFK come to think of it; have absolutely no connection to Malta. The same bullet thing must be a mistake.'

'I see. Tell me Thea, where did you pick the last envelope up from?'

'Outside Villa Blye in Paola.'

'And do you know what Villa Blye is?'

'No.'

'A Masonic Temple……and the "bullet thing" is no mistake.'

*

Spiteri was happy when her landline rang: *I need a break from this.* 'I need to go Hunter; bye. Hello, Sarah.'

'Sorry to call you at home but your mobile was engaged for an eternity.'

'Don't ask. What is it?'

'Do you remember that you asked me to get some of the older officers to think over where men might be held for a long time?' asked Said.

'Yes…..nothing came out of it, though.'

'Well, a Constable Nichols got back to me. He has come up with a theory.'

'Which is?'

'You know the story of the Odyssey; about Ulysses being held captive by a woman called "Calypso." '

'Vaguely.'

'Well, Ulysses was held for seven years apparently …… and there are exactly seven-year gaps between our missing men. He thinks we have a modern day Calypso.'

'A bit far-fetched don't you think, Sarah?'

'Yes and No. Pace and Muscat were held for long periods.'

'Even so…..'

'He said he would like to do a little research; maybe come up with an idea.'

'That's fine. Contact his Sergeant and tell him I want this guy seconded to us for a couple of days.'

'OK…will do.'

*

Miriam Zammit's final day as a Magistrate was not going to be a happy one. Her initial sadness at the fact that it was her last day, had been dispelled by the knowledge that she still had other, perhaps even more important, roles to play.

But the arrival of Chief Justice Emeritus: George Bonnici, in her chambers before the start of the day's proceedings set off every alarm bell that Zammit had.

'Miriam, how are you; very nice to see you again. Will you be attending our rather belated New Year Dinner tonight?'

'George, I know you don't find it remotely nice to see me, and couldn't give a rat's arse if I attended the dinner. What do you want?'

'Come, come Miriam.....some measure of decorum, please! We are in the Courts after all.'

'Shit. Right, once again: what do you want, George?'

'Have it your way, Miriam. Defence Council will submit a motion for the Grech case to be dismissed this morning. You will agree to that.'

'I will not.'

'Miriam, you will.....that is my instruction.'

'On what grounds?'

'National security interests.'

'Ah....he's fucking the Defence Minister's wife then?'

'You really are awfully crude Miriam; just as well you are moving on I think.'

'I won't do it.'

'You will do it.'

'Or?'

'Or, you will be taken off the case, the case will be dismissed anyway.....and your pension entitlement will be reviewed.'

'Ah, blackmail.....your strong point by all accounts.'

'Goodbye Magistrate Zammit, I can't say it's been a pleasure.'

*

'Dom Perignon and keep it coming young man!'

Michael Grech and some colleagues who hadn't abandoned him for his "little indiscretions" were set on a night of champagne, cocaine and lap dancers: 'I have some catching up to do boys!' Michael Grech would indeed enjoy champagne and cocaine that night, but it would be him who was caught up

with.

*

Spiteri decided to pop into her old office to see how things were progressing, and for a bit of nostalgia. On the way there she noticed she had a Voicemail on her mobile: 'Superintendent, your next envelope can be found at the entrance to Florida Mansions on Triq Enrico Mizzi, Ta Xbiex. It will be on the table there at 9.00 pm this evening; collect it before 9.05 pm.' *Yes, Sir….right away Sir….Christ.*

Said was seated at her desk when Spiteri came in: 'Oh, hello, I didn't expect to see you.'

'I'm a "Mystery Customer!" Is Raul not here?'

'He is but about an hour ago he got a call from Immigration about some African guy that they had arrested at the airport. He's down in one of the Interview rooms talking to him.'

'Why, what's Immigration got to do with us?'

'No idea really; Raul didn't say anything, but to be fair I don't think he knew himself.'

'Strange.'

The phone on Said's desk rang. Said answered it, listened for a few moments, then said: 'Superintendent Spiteri is here; should she come too?'; then, after a short pause: 'OK.'

'That was Inspector Mifsud; he says we need to come down to the Interview Room.'

Spiteri and Said entered the Interview Room a few minutes later. Mifsud and the Immigration Officer were sitting at a desk opposite a nervous looking man, dressed in ill-fitting and dirty clothes.

'Ma'am, this is Jafar Nimeiri. He has been working and living in one of the maintenance hangars at the Airport for the last 4 or 5 months; he's not sure how long. He's here illegally, and his English isn't good, but he managed to get across to Immigration that he had important information that he would trade if he could stay on Malta, and his wife and daughter are allowed to join him. I told him we couldn't guarantee anything, but that he would definitely be deported if he didn't talk.'

'OK, and what has he told you?' asked Spiteri.

'Not so much told us, more shown us. OK Jafar, show us again' said Mifsud, motioning with his hand for the man to get up, and nodding his head encouragingly. Jafar smiled enthusiastically and jumped to his feet.

Jafar then held his arms out and ran towards the room wall, pretending to smash into it. He then held up one finger, and shook his head. He then held up two fingers, and nodded. He indicated the Nos Two again, lifted his satchel, put it over his shoulder and climbed up on his chair.....and jumped off.

Mifsud looked up at Spiteri; she had already worked it out.

'Mother of God! There were two people on the planes.....one parachuted out.'

*

Back upstairs in the Homicide Squad room; Spiteri sat with Mifsud and Said.

'Right, the Restins. Helen Restin has been staying with me over the holidays. She appears to be a lovely woman who is genuinely devastated at the loss of her husband and son. I don't think that she is involved in any way, but a couple of things she has said have made me think that her late husband, and possibly son, had powerful enemies. The information from Jafar makes it look like there was a second person on each flight who parachuted out before the planes crashed. I've been in one of those planes before, so you can take my word that the "passenger" couldn't have been "hiding" and surprised the victims. No; the victims willingly let the guy or girl I suppose, onto the plane. I'm guessing that they then reached a certain height; the "passenger" smashes the pilot over the head; who is going to know that a bash on the head hadn't happened when the plane crashed?..........he then jumps out. Simple plan really.

So, who would want the Restins killed? Who even knew they were here in Malta? What were they doing in Malta in the first place? I know about the cruise thing, but were they here for any other reason? But, Raul, I want you to assign that work out initially, I'll see you get body numbers to help. First thing to arrange is a sketch artist and interpreter to sit with Jafar Nimeiri.'

'OK.'

*

One minute after 9.00 pm Thea Spiteri lifted a familiar-looking type of envelope from the table that stood just where Hunter said it would. Her hands were shaking slightly and the blood had drained from her face. A moment earlier she had realised that she was at the entrance to a synagogue.

*

By 10.30 pm Spiteri was opening a second bottle of wine. She hadn't opened the latest envelope, and was beginning to wish that she hadn't opened the first. *I must confront Hunter, this is all.......*

Spiteri's mobile rang, the screen was blank: 'Good evening, Hunter.'

'Good evening, Thea....I trust you are well?' said the now familiar voice.

'Depressed would be closer to the truth.'

'Oh; why?'

'The world is a terrible place.'

'Then we must endeavour to change that. I take it that we now 'agree' that President Kennedy was assassinated by three professional hit men. These men were recruited by the CIA through connections that the Mafia had in France. Also, the number of Freemasons who play active roles in the story is beyond question.'

'Only partially; I find the CIA being involved in the killing of their own President a bit difficult to accept.'

'OK...let me enlighten you. The CIA's involvement was 'fronted' by CIA Agent Cord Meyer; whose wife was having an affair with Kennedy at the time. The CIA acted in collaboration with the Federal Reserve Bank [the paymasters] on the orders of a cabal that was formed for the sole purpose of killing Kennedy.

So....we return to 1963. There is a very intricate and complicated financial strategy being put in place by Kennedy. Suffice to say that it involves eliminating the power of the Federal Reserve Bank and replacing it with a 'new' dollar, issued by the US Government, and underwritten by its gold reserves. Unsurprisingly, this did not please the Federal Reserve Bank one bit.'

'But hold on a minute; what is the big difference in the two systems?'

'The difference, Thea....and not many people actually realise this; is that the Federal Reserve Bank is neither Federal nor a Reserve Bank. It is a private banking conglomerate owned by the Rothschild and Rockefeller cabals. As I said, the strategy Kennedy wanted to pursue was very complicated and had to be taken in stages. However, progress was being made, and on 14th Nov 1963 Kennedy signed something called the Green Hilton Memorial Agreement which was an important milestone in him being able to fulfil his vision. Six days later, in Mexico; remember Mexico from our previous conversations: Antoine Guerini and Lucien Sarti finalised their plans. The following day, as I've already said, the three gunmen crossed the border into Texas; where they were picked up by Chicago Mob driver and bag man; Frank Marcello.

The next day they shot Kennedy and on the 26th Nov, they were escorted into Canada.'

Being an excellent Pulizija officer you will no doubt have picked up on the fact that Sarti, Oswald and Hunt were all in Mexico City before the shootings?....and the boat commissioned to take the killers out of Canada was paid for by a company registered in Mexico City…..and that Meyer's boss in the CIA was…..'

'The Freemason…..Howard Hunt. Fuck.'

'What do you make of the new information you picked up?'

'Nothing, I haven't read it yet; but I've a feeling that I don't need to be Sherlock Holmes to know what it implies.'

'It doesn't 'imply' anything; it merely states facts. Read it, I'll call you back in 20 minutes.'

'20 minutes?'

'Time is running out Thea.'

Spiteri looked down at the envelope, sipped at her refilled glass of wine…..and opened the envelope.

List of 33rd Degree Masons [NB Thea – this is the highest Masonic rank there is]

The Rothschild dynasty

The Rockefeller dynasty

Yitzhak Rabin

Earl Warren

J Edgar Hoover

L B Johnson

Bush x 3

G Ford

<u>Jack Ruby</u>
Real Name : Jack Rubinstein
Soldier in Dallas Mafia

Nov 21st, 1963 – [day before assassination] – JR visits Lamar Hunt [brother of Howard Hunt] – Watergate conspirator

Nov 22nd, 1963 – JFK assassinated 12.30 pm – 12.35 pm JR photographed standing outside the Texas Book Depository

Nov 22nd, 1963 – Seth Kantor, a reporter who knew JR personally; gives a statement that he met and spoke to JR in Parkland Hospital – the hospital where JFK was taken and the infamous "magic bullet" was found. The Warren Committee were given the statement, and ignored it.

Nov 22nd, 1963 – 7.00 pm – JR seen at; and spoken to, by several police officers who knew him, the Dallas Police Dept building where Oswald was being held. Jr was openly carrying a gun.

Nov 22nd, 1963 – JR attends Friday night service at his local synagogue

Nov 24th, 1963 – Jack Rubenstein shoots and kills Oswald. The Warren Commission later asserts that there was no conspiracy involved in the killing of Lee Harvey Oswald.

*

Exactly 20 minutes after his first call, Hunter rang back. Before he spoke, Spiteri took the initiative: 'I don't think Jews; like Catholics, can be Masons?'

'Well, you are clearly wrong there. If I may quote from one of my favourite films "The Magnificent 7"….. "now we have 6."'

'What?'

'Groups Thea, groups. CIA; FBI; Freemasons; Jews; Bankers; political opponents.'

'Will we get 7?'

'Yes….and that is not even counting the occult. We'll talk later. Oh, incidentally, was the airport cleaner of any use to you?'

'What? Occult….wait….that was you?'

'His story is true, I merely persuaded him to talk to you. I told him you were a very compassionate woman.'

'Look, this is……'

Hunter was gone.

Chapter Twenty

The Redemption of Ulysses

Friday 15th
Floriana
9.00 am
Spiteri had only been in her office for a few minutes when her phone rang; it was Raul Mifsud. 'Ma'am can we come and see you; it's important?'

'We?'

'Yes, I have Constable Nichols here.'

'OK, come over now.'

Mifsud and Nichols were both seated across from Spiteri about 10 minutes later.

'Ma'am, you'll remember Constable Nichols here had come up with a theory about what was behind the Missing Men issues?'

'Yes, a modern day Calypso.'

'That's right but at that time, he couldn't come up with any likely location for where the men could be held. Obviously, you know the 'Calypso Cave' on Gozo.'

'Yes, of course…..but they can't possibly be there!'

'No, but a number of years ago, just down from the cave, someone tried to build a huge luxury hotel.'

'Yes, I know it….I've been there a few times. The men can't be there Raul. There are couples; tourists swarming all over it practically every day.'

'Yes I know…..but what I didn't know, till now, was that the reason the hotel became derelict was that it was built on clay. Very soon after construction, and some rain, the hotel slipped down the hillside and was condemned.'

'OK, but I'm still not getting……'

'The point is that when the whole project was abandoned, someone bought the land. It was very cheap as it's not of much use for anything.'

'I'm still not…..'

'The land was bought by a company. They are registered in Switzerland; I can't find out much about them; apart from their name.'

'Which is?'

'Herodotus 14.'

'And that should interest me because……..'

'Well, it didn't seem significant to me either Ma'am; but our resident 'Officer Homer' here was in the Bibliotheca last night, and had a brain-wave. It's not Herodotus 14; it's Herodotus 1.4: a quote from Greek mythology.'

'Which says?'

Mifsud read from his notebook: 'It reads; "To be anxious to avenge rape is foolish; wise men take no notice of such things. For plainly the women would never have been carried away, had they not wanted it themselves."

'Very enlightened…..but Raul it is men who are missing; not women.'

'Yes, but remember that as well as the miss-ing men, there were numbers of men who were missing for a short period….and when they returned they had been emasculated in some way.'

'So…..what you are suggesting is that a woman is keeping these men captive?'

'Not just any woman, Ma'am…..Calypso…..she was the Goddess of

Concealment. It's true that she fell in love with Ulysses, but she was also a Siren…the sea nymphs who lured men to their deaths with their singing.'

'It's really intriguing Raul but I can't base an investigation on it.'

'Ma'am, the hotel slipped down; but the cellars and stores, which were underground, stayed where they were and were just covered over. What if someone found a way in?'

'God, it's possible I suppose. I'm still not…..'

'Ma'am, neither was I so I dug out the original plans for the hotel. There was an underground level of 20 rooms…..numbered 70 to 90.'

'86…..Christ…..they were named after room numbers.'

*

Spiteri was stunned to find out that no sonar or heat-seeking equipment was available on the island. 'What would we do if there was an earthquake or a tsunami?'

'Shout?' was Mifsud's unhelpful reply.

Ten-year-old Rosa Munn had spent the last hour watching the men and women wandering around the area she usually played on while her mother sold lace to the tourists visiting "Calypso Cave." She was under strict instructions not to talk to strangers, but she knew that some of these people were Pulizija officers and so thought her mother wouldn't mind. Anyway, her mother had always told her she should be kind and help people. Rosa wandered down the hill to where the pretty lady with the very dark hair stood watching over things and sometimes talking on her phone.

'Have you lost your ball?' asked Rosa.

'Oh hello, what's your name?' replied Spiteri.

'Rosa. Have you lost your ball?'

'No, not a ball, but we have lost some things.'

'What kind of things?'

'Oh, just different things. We think they might have fallen under the broken building.'

'Mm. Are they big things?'

'Yes….quite big.'

'Well, they can't have fallen through the cracks then.'

'No, that's right. Clever girl.'

'My mum says I'm a Princess, I pretend this is my palace.'

'Your mum is right; you are a beautiful Princess.'

'I think I'll go for a drink now, I'm thirsty.'

'OK, it was nice chatting with you, Rosa. Bye.'

'Bye.'

Rosa turned and started to walk off: 'If it's big things you're looking for you should maybe try the round door. Bye.'

'Rosa….wait! Where is the round door, can you show me?'

'OK, but I can't stay.'

'That's OK…..you show me where the round door is and I will get a Pulizija man to take you home and tell your mum how good you have been…..and I'll give you 5 euros for sweets.'

On first sight, all that the little girl had led them to was an overgrown corner of what had once been a courtyard: 'Squeeze behind the bushes, watch out for spiders, though.'

Spiteri pushed through the undergrowth but at first, couldn't see any doors, never mind a round one. *I think Rosa has been watching too many Hobbit films.* She turned to push her way back out and heard a hollow sound from where she put her foot down. Spiteri cleared the area with her foot. A round well cover sat staring back at her; a modern padlock gleaming in the sun.

An hour passed whilst a team of officers were assembled with ropes, torches and, in hope, medical equipment. A doctor and two nurses had also been brought in.

Spiteri's hands covered her mouth as; a half hour later, a bedraggled wreck of a man was pulled from the well: 'Keep his eyes well covered' shouted the doctor. 'Get him to the ambulance as quick as you can.' The man's long hair was grey, with red tinges. The ambulance sped off and Spiteri was called to the top of the well: 'that seems to be it in terms of anyone alive, but hell has been unleashed in this place Ma'am......hell on earth.'

Spiteri called Commissioner Malia on her way to the hospital and told him what had happened.

'My God, that's unbelievable.'

'I know, poor man. I'm on my way to the hospital if that's OK; I need to try and speak to him, I feel a responsibility. I'm not expecting anything; he probably won't know much.

'Yes, that's fine.'

Spiteri was about to enter the hospital when her phone rang.

'Miriam, nice to hear from you.'

'Thea, I warned you that you were on my list! Can we meet for lunch today......I'm a "Lady who does lunch" now.'

'Really, what happened in Grech case?'

'I'll tell you at lunch if that's OK; my blood is still boiling at the moment.'

'OK. I'm just going into Mater Dei to speak to someone, but could meet you at 1.00 pm in, say, Niño's?'

'Perfect, see you then.'

*

Thea Spiteri heard; Red O'Toole before she saw him: 'It is not a rat, it is my friend!'

'I don't care if it's your cousin; you are not keeping a rat with you, and that's final.'

'What if I tell him not to speak?'

'I'll be telling you not to speak shortly. Nurse, take that animal and release it outside…..now!'

'Farwell, Ithaca, you shall be forever in my heart!'

Spiteri was taken aback at how strong, healthy and in apparently good spirits O'Toole was.

'Peter, my name is Superintendent Spiteri, but I was a mere Constable when I was on the team searching for you all those years ago. I'm so pleased you've now been found.'

'Ladies are always late; it is their prerogative.'

'Peter, can you tell us what happened; how you were taken?'

'I can't Madam. One minute I was heading for my breakfast; the next I was chained to an industrial oven! Oh, the irony!'

'You seem remarkably well for someone who has just been through what you have.'

'Superintendent, it is all an illusion. I am not well, in fact, I am probably dying, but I refused to do so for that harlot.'

'Who Peter, who is the harlot?'

'Her name.....who knows? Her profession?.....inflicting pain.'

'Can you describe her?'

'In detail my dear, in detail. Every line and wisp of her hair are embedded in my brain.'

'Once you have been fully checked by the doctors, can I bring a sketch artist in, get you to give her everything on the harlot's appearance.'

'Certainly, but not till Monday.'

'Monday!'

'Absolutely. I checked with the nurse in the ambulance; today is Friday....and it is 2016. Tonight I will sleep, and in the morning I'm off to Malachy's to bring in a New Year; for me at least.....and a new beginning.'

'Are you serious?'

'Absolutely......don't you think I've wasted enough weekends?'

'Well, when you look at it that way. You are a remarkable man Red.'

'Remarkable...No....alive....Yes.....that is the point. See you on Monday fair lady.'

*

'You look very pleased, Thea!' said Miriam Zammit.

'I am……delighted in fact.'

'Do tell.'

'It's unbelievable actually, but listen to this. Many years ago, over 20 in fact, I was involved in a Missing Person case; a man called O'Toole.'

'Irish I assume!'

'Yes. Anyway, and you won't know anything about this, nobody did until a few weeks ago; but over the years other men have been going missing, never to be seen again. However, one did turn up recently, bewildered and filthy but, to cut a long story short, things he said led us to a place up in Gozo where these men were being held. We raided it this morning…. Guess what?'

'What?'

'My missing man was there…..and alive!'

'My God, that is unbelievable.'

'I know, and even better, he's lucid. He seems to have been able to deal with his situation and, even better, he's agreed to sit with an artist on Monday…..do an I.D. of his captor…..who, believe it or not, is a woman!'

'Good God in heaven. But why wait till Monday?'

'The man is a real character! He insists he's spending the weekend in Malachy's bar in Marsascala….bringing in 2016 with his best friend.'

'His best friend?'

'Yes…..Guinness.'

Both women laughed – 'Ah, the Irish, hometown boys, eh Thea!'

'I know. So; what about your news?'

'A bad news story to compete with your good news one I'm afraid.'

'Why what's happened?'

'You'll have heard of, maybe even met, that snake of a man; George Bonnici?'

'The Chief Justice…..or whatever they call themselves these days?'

'Exactly. He sauntered into my Chambers this morning and basically told me to release a rapist.'

'What…Why?….Are you talking about Grech?'

'Yes. A question of national security apparently. Complete rubbish of course. Grech must have something on him or someone else in power. Prostitutes, or boys, is my guess.'

'How disgusting, what are we even doing in the "Justice Business" Miriam?'

'Well, I'm not now!'

'No….more's the pity. What now for you Miriam…..the world is your oyster so they say!'

'Well I do have a couple of "justice" issues to clear up actually. But they can wait, because tonight I am going to a belated New Year Party at the Law Society Club tonight – I intend to get very drunk, tell Bonnici; my Hermes, exactly what I think of him and then sleep all weekend.'

'An excellent plan Miriam……I may follow your lead…..without the confrontation bit!'

*

7.00 pm Friday
Spiteri's home

That evening, Thea Spiteri did indeed follow her friend Miriam's lead: feet up, tuna salad and a few glasses of wine with Helen. Helen had told her that she was going to go back to the States.

'I know I said I wouldn't leave the bodies here, Thea, but I've got to be practical…..all these investigations could take a year to get to court.'

'I understand, it must be terrible for you. When will you go?'

'I've booked a flight for Monday the 25th. I'll return my car, and take the Courtesy Car from the Hilton to the airport.'

'I'll miss you, Helen. I've enjoyed having you here. If only the circumstances had been different.'

'I know. I feel the same. Obviously, I'll be back in Malta; maybe we can have more sociable outings then, or you could always visit the States. I would pay everything; I'm exceptionally rich now apparently.'

Thea Spiteri knew that Helen wasn't rich in the way she wanted: 'Thank you......we'll see.'

'So, what are your plans for the weekend?'

'Right now, I'm going to go out for a walk, then an early night if that's OK with you. Saturday and Sunday hopefully we can spend some time sight-seeing or a nice meal out; a lunch.....something.'

Despite the wine and the avoidance of all 'depressing' chat, Spiteri couldn't contemplate going to bed at the same time as Helen. Apart from the 'earlyish' hour; things were eating away at the back of her mind. She pulled over her laptop that was lying on the couch beside her. She brought up 'Google' and typed in 'Calypso.' Sirens, sea nymphs and visions of Brad Pitt in the film "Troy," filled her head: *"....and Zeus, after being persuaded by Athena, sent Hermes, the Messenger of the Gods; to instruct Calypso to set Odysseus free."*

Spiteri's brow furrowed; a few minutes passed, Spiteri decided to call Said even though she knew Said wasn't on call that weekend: 'Sarah, sorry to call when you're off.'

'That's OK; I'm on my way out actually, you've just caught me.'

'Oh, where are you off to?'

'Promise you won't laugh?'

'Don't be silly….tell me!'

'Evening classes…..I'm studying Greek Mythology…..I've always been interested in it; from my teens actually, but never went into it in depth. Listening to Nichols got me moving again. Anyway, is anything wrong?'

'That's great, Sarah, well done you. Sarah, can you remember where Ramon Pace was found?'

'Yes, he was wandering about in a daze in Ramla village on Gozo. Why?'

'Think this over; how did he get there? How did he even get out of the well?'

'I suppose he…….'

'He was set free, Sarah. He didn't escape; he was set free…..just like Odysseus.'

'In that case, why wasn't Red set free after 7 years; and the others?'

'Because they died before they could be……all except Red.'

'OK, so why wasn't Red set free?'

'I'm guessing it's because he wasn't a "broken" man. She knew if she let him go, he could identify her.'

'I suppose we'll have a better idea on Monday; he's a bit of a character isn't he…..wanting to go to his old pub!'

'He certainly is. Have a good time, Sarah. I'll see you on Monday.'

Spiteri had always liked Said, they had become friends. She hoped that she would one day find the love that seemed to have eluded her till now…..*have that baby girl…..what was it she was going to call her again….ah yes…..little Athena.*

Time stood still: *Christ no, please God no!*

Spiteri hated herself for what she was thinking: *it's just not possible. What can I do? I can't speak to anyone else until I'm certain. Please don't let this be real. Think Thea, think! Wait….she's out tonight….I could…..*

Less than half an hour later; Spiteri had drawn up outside her friend's door: *You're out of your mind doing this, Thea. Police Officers aren't supposed to break-in to people's homes….you must do it Thea…you must rule out any suspicions you have….. Christ, sometimes being in the Pulizija is a curse.*

191

Spiteri viewed the home as "simple and tasteful" had she been an Estate Agent. *What exactly are you looking for Thea?*

Spiteri never answered herself for the simple reason that as she wandered from room to room there was absolutely nothing that triggered her imagination. Spiteri decided to exit the house through the back door from the kitchen; she smiled at the scene of neat and tidy domesticity; even down to the chalk message board on the wall displaying her shopping list: pot's lemon lime.

Spiteri started to drive home with a strange mixture of relief....and annoyance at herself for seeing ghosts in every corner. Stopped at a traffic light she glanced at a road sign: Marsascala 1 Klm: *Right Thea, let's have a look at this bar that holds such an attraction for Red!*

A few minutes later, as Thea Spiteri drove past the front of Malachy's; all her fears returned.

Saturday Morning
Marsascala

Thea Spiteri chose her spot carefully. She had made sure she was the first customer in Malachy's. She ordered a coffee and picked a seat where she could observe the whole bar, but could not be seen by people entering.

At 11.00 am a cleaned-up, but somehow more broken looking, Peter O'Toole entered the bar. His beaming smile as he ordered a pint of Guinness, soon disappearing as he realised that the world had moved on: no-one knew Peter O'Toole now; no-one except the next customer.

Miriam Zammit hesitated momentarily as a waitress passed with a drink for a customer sitting outside. Once alone, she stepped forward, and Spiteri could see the thin stiletto blade in her hand.

'Don't do it, Miriam.'

Zammit's body went rigid at the sound of her name; and the realisation of who was speaking. She turned and looked into the darkened seating alcove.

'Thea.'

'Miriam, come and sit down; it's over.'

Zammit did as she was instructed to do, even laying the knife on the table for Spiteri.

'I'm glad in a way, Thea. How did you know I'd be here?'

'You called Bonnici "Hermes"….it got me thinking; and…..'

'And?'

'And I broke into your house when you were at the Law Society…..I saw your Food List. Except it wasn't a food list was it, Miriam? It wasn't potatoes, lemons and limes……it was short for "Peter O'Toole at Lemon & Lime"….the new name for Malachy's.'

'Very good, Thea. I always knew you were smart.'

'Why Miriam; my God, why?'

'Why? Justice Thea; that is why. I chose to study Law because, by the time I was ready for University, I already knew that there was no justice.'

'You'll have to explain what you mean.'

'Does the name Josef Calleja mean anything to you, Thea?'

'Josef Calleja…..I've heard it somewhere, but…..'

'It will be in your files under Missing.'

'Yes, 1970's…..he's the first who never returned.'

'That's right……and he never will.'

'Miriam, I think……'

'Lawyer?…ha….I am a lawyer. Let me talk…..I want to talk…..for the first time…..I want to talk. In 1973 I was an innocent girl, a happy girl. I took a lift to school from a neighbour.'

'Calleja?'

'Exactly. We never got to school that day. He raped me in the back of his van. One week later, I stood at the same bus stop and smiled at Calleja as he drove past. He stopped: 'I know a nice place in Gozo if you would like a picnic' I said. My father was an architect; I knew about the "moving hotel."

'So you took him there?'

'Yes; I even let him take me again.'

'Why?'

'Because he was a disgusting fat pig who fell asleep after any exertion. Only this time, when he woke up, he was mine.'

'You killed him?'

'No! Nothing so crude, Thea. I kept him.'

'Kept him?'

'Yes. I meant it to be for 7 years, like the Odyssey, but he died.'

'When, how many years was he there?'

'Four.'

'Four! You were only 17, how did you do it?'

'When he woke up he was chained up and secure.....and he had no tongue or eyes. He was grateful to be alive.'

Then, in 1978 my father died. I got a small inheritance and used it to buy the site.

Spiteri studied Zammit: *can this be true?*

'But Miriam, Calypso loved Ulysses.....she didn't torture him.'

'Yes, but Calleja denied me the ability to love. I have no regrets, Thea.'

'But what about the others, they were innocent?'

'Innocent? Really, check their records. All guilty of violating girls....all set free. I made sure justice was done. I'm just sorry you've stopped me; Grech was next on my list.'

'You'll have to come with me, Miriam. I'm sorry.'

'Don't be, you are only doing what you have to do.......like I did.'

Thea Spiteri handed Miriam Zammit over to the duty officer in Floriana, with a heavy heart.

*

After handing Miriam over to the Desk Sergeant, Spiteri went up to the Homicide Office. Being a Saturday afternoon, she wasn't sure anyone would be there, so she was pleased to see Said sitting at her desk.

'Sarah, I want you to check the criminal histories of the Missing Men.'

Said wasn't quite sure why she was being asked to do the checks, as she was unaware of Zammit's arrest.

'OK, anything in particular?'

'No, I just want to clear up something in my head' said Spiteri as she headed for the door.

The phone on Said's desk rang.

Said motioned for Spiteri to stop: 'Ma'am, you won't believe this?'

'What?'

'Michael Grech has been reported missing.'

*

Sunday Morning

Spiteri was happy that Peter O'Toole was alive, but wondered if the disappointment she saw on his face in "Lemon and Lime" on that Saturday morning would ever fade. *Poor man....what a terrible life he's had.* It was also great that all the related murders were solved, and the relatives of the "Missing" would have some degree of satisfaction. There and then Spiteri decided to befriend Red O'Toole; to help him slowly integrate back into society, and if that meant sitting in Malachy's: *then so be it Thea...you might even like this craic thing the Irish are always talking about.* Spiteri's mobile rang.

*

Sunday Afternoon

Adrianne Valetta enjoyed her 'lazy' Sundays. No work, nice lunch, Sunday papers. She was particularly enjoying this Sunday after reading in the Malta Times that a woman Magistrate had been arrested for abducting and torturing men.

*

Spiteri had been a little surprised when Jack Carter had called her and asked if she would like to join him and Clark for a "Traditional English Sunday Lunch"....' a throw-back to the glory days of Empire I believe! No strings or expectations; a few drinks....nice meal....no CIA talk!'

Spiteri was glad she had accepted. Carter was interesting company; if not really 'her type' looks wise. *What exactly is your type, Thea; Matt and Nicola aren't exactly similar. Change the subject Thea....now!*

Bill Clark was a different proposition; Spiteri found the chair she was sitting in more interesting than him

'Did you always want to be in law enforcement then, Jack?'

'Not really. I was a typical college kid....bit of pot, too much beer, too few girls.....no idea what I was doing, where I was going. I drifted into it really. What about you?'

'Yes, I always wanted to be in the Puliz-ija.....joined at 18.'

'So not that long ago then?'

'Flattery will get you everywhere Agent Carter! What about you Bill?'

'I wanted to be a Marine, didn't get in; but I'm still serving my country, that's all I care about.'

'Right.........so who do you think killed JFK, Bill?'

'Muslims and gays.'

'What.....in 1963?'

'You saying they weren't around then?'

'No...it's just that.....'

'Listen, Christianity is the only answer.....end of.'

'A lot of priests and ministers are gay.'

'Not in my church they ain't.'

'Live and let live I say; I don't see why the USA thinks it has to 'Police' the world, imposing its views. Your way is not the only way; you know.'

'And what is 'our' way, Ma'am?'

'White, middle-class Christians, all the 'right' college boys enticed into serving their nation....no offence but the word clones comes to mind. Sorry.' Thea Spiteri even manages to suppress a smile as she notices both men wearing the same Alma Mater rings....*they don't even realise....*

'Oh that ain't 'our way' Ma'am....that's God's way.'

Christ Thea.......change the subject.

'Any of you guys ever tasted our local beer; Cisk?'

'No thank you, I only drink on Christmas Day.'

'Truly?'

'Yea, two drinks & he's under the stable!' said Carter.

'I don't like jokes involving religion Jack……..you know that.'

'Quite right too; if I were you I'd go out & kill the first born of every comedian in the land; that would teach them.'

Clark stood: 'I think I'll leave you guys to enjoy the rest of the day.' Clark walked off after throwing a 20 euro note onto the table.

'Well….that's that then!

'Yea; sorry about Bill, he's "Born Again" Christian.'

'Don't think "Christian" is the word I'd use.'

'So; what were you studying at college, Jack?'

'Business! I saw myself as a Bill Gates type! The American Dream thing, a bit like that Massa guy you asked about.'

'Oh yeah, I meant to ask: what business is he in?'

'He owns a chain of Flying and Sky Diving Schools right across the States.'

Spiteri tried not to let Carter see that she had slumped into the chair. 'Jack, I've really enjoyed today, thank you for inviting me, but I have a really early start tomorrow, I'll need to get going. Thank you so much for the lovely meal.'

'My pleasure, nothing bad in the morning I hope?'

'So do I Jack. Jack....can you do one last thing for me?'

'Sure, if I can.'

'Remember a while back you told me you had a list of Corsican names that were of interest in the JFK shooting?'

'Yea.'

'Could you send me a copy of the list?'

'Thea, I'll do everything within my power to help you, but if I find out you've been duping me........'

'I'm not, Jack. It's a hunch that's all. If I see any connection, I promise I'll share everything with you.'

'The name Massa is not on the list.'

'OK, but can I see it anyway.'

'Not really; not on my say so, I'm not high enough up on the food chain.'

'How can I get them?'

'Tell me why you want them; it's a trust issue; are you working with us, or for yourself.'

'Jack, you know my personal situation; but, I can assure you….I'm a police officer first. Can you get me the list?'

'No need.'

'What?'

'No need……I have the names in my head.'

'Really? How have you managed that?'

'Not difficult Inspector; there are only two names on it.'

'And they are…….'

'Sarti and Basti'

'Basti………as in the name of the Corsican capital?'

'Yes, you've seen "The Godfather" haven't you…..the Corleone family? It isn't uncommon with migrants; they try to fit in with their new culture.'

'Sure, there certainly seems to be a lot of that goes on with migrant families. I need to go…… and, Jack……'

'What?'

'Thanks.'

Within a few minutes, Spiteri was sitting in her car, going through her emails. She hadn't bothered opening the Massa picture attachment Carter had sent days before; once she heard that he had no criminal record. She opened it, and then called Said:

'Do you have the artist's impression of the plane jumper handy, Sarah?'

'Yes, it's on my phone.'

'Can you email me it straight away?'

'OK.'

'And you got Jafar to sign that this was a good likeness?'

'Yes…..ish.'

'What do you mean?'

'He signed it with initials, I suppose he can't write.'

'That's still OK…..his whole name I take it?'

'Well it looked like DBG to me, but his writing is weird.'

'Doesn't matter, as long as he recognises it. OK send it now please.'

The email arrived on Spiteri's phone within seconds: *No mistaking that Thea….Pietru is the guy Jafar saw. He would have had no problem getting into the planes….he probably just said that 'The Bosses' wanted tightened security. It wouldn't be suspicious about him being there; given the "business" aspect of their own trips. Fuck, what now Thea?*

'Sarah, do you happen to know anything about Freemasonry?'

'Not really. It's some sort of secret boys club I think; quasi -religious, business, the occult.....all sorts.'

'The occult; how did you know that?'

'Don't laugh but my Aunt claims to speak to the dead; does séances, Tarot reading....the lot.'

'Can you bring her to my office at 10.00 am tomorrow?'

'What?.......seriously?'

'Very. See you tomorrow.'

*

Sunday Evening

Peter O'Toole strolled in the early evening sun, enjoying the feel of freedom on his face. He reached the far side of St Thomas Bay; San Tomas, to the locals, and followed the steep path around the headland to the next bay. At that height, the slight breeze and uninterrupted view into eternity made a picture perfect setting. Red stepped off the cliff, and entered his own eternity.

Chapter Twenty-One

Monday morning
Spiteri's Office
Floriana
Monday 11.00 am

The following morning Spiteri was sitting at her desk musing as to what the "White Witch" might look like. *Definitely long dirty hair; dirty fingernails, probably a stoop, will definitely have warts on her face…..if she comes in holding a wand Thea…..run!*

A knock on her door indicated she would soon know: 'Come in.'

Sarah Said entered along with a woman of similar age to Spiteri. She was immaculately dressed in a business suit that Spiteri would struggle to afford, and she had perfectly cared for hair and nails.

Spiteri's eyes darted to Said: *there must be a mix-up.*

Before Said could speak, the business-like woman offered Spiteri her hand: 'Good morning, Superintendent. Jan Gauci; or Elm Wood, if you want to use my coven name! I could tell from your confused look that you thought that my niece Sarah had brought the wrong Aunt.'

'No, no....not at all...I, eh, was just.....'

'It's OK Superintendent.....it happens a lot.'

'Please, call me Thea.....take a seat. Sarah, I'm sorry to do this but I'm afraid I can't let you sit-in.....this is linked to the Sarstedt killing.'

'That's fine; I didn't think it related to any-thing the team was working on. Aunt Jan find me when you're finished and I'll take you back to work.'

The 'team' barb was not lost on Spiteri....*fuck....live with it, Sarah.*

'So Jan, where do you work?'

'I'm an Accountant for HSBC in St Julians.'

'Really, I thought......'

'Oh, I know....interested in the occult....must be a weirdo.'

'Well......'

'Don't worry; if you think about it, it all makes sense. Numbers play a very important role in the occult....and accountancy!'

Spiteri had taken an instant liking to Jan Gauci: 'Jan, what we are about to talk about cannot leave this room; not even to Sarah.'

'I understand.'

'OK. I am working on a very complicated case at the moment and a remark was made by one of my colleagues regarding a possible 'occult' involvement. I was wondering if you could throw some light on how that might show itself?'

'Thea, the occult is all numbers and symbols. I could give you a quick general overview but that wouldn't really help you in a specific case. I would need to know what numbers and symbols you're talking about.'

'I understand.....I think! OK, this will sound strange I know but I'm interested in any occult rumours surrounding the assassination of President Kennedy in 1963.'

Spiteri wasn't sure what sort of reaction she would get from someone when a Pulizija officer in Malta asked about a 50-year-old case in the

USA; but the one she got took her aback: Jan Gauci started to laugh.

'JFK….Thea, it's a classic occult influenced case. The proof is incontrovertible….to believers. Do you want a shortened version?'

'Yes please.'

'JFK was everything the 'establishment' didn't want. Catholic, charismatic, non-mason…committed to 'taming' the South and the anti-black disgraces going on down there. The only reason he got in was because the Mafia were under the illusion that he would leave them alone and he was anti- Vietnam war too…..the Peace Movement and Martin Luther King etc were on the rise. It was a perfect storm for him. Anyways, it didn't take long for the Mafia to find out they were wrong and, even worse in the 'establish-ments' eyes, he was going to scrap the Federal Reserve Bank……he had to go.'

'Are you saying a group of 'Devil Wor-shipers' did it? '

'No….any and everyone who was affected by what JFK was doing, and who love symbolism, got together and did it.'

'How does that manifest itself in the JFK killing?'

'Well it couldn't be clearer:

Kennedy was shot and killed in Dealey Plaza in Dallas, Texas on 22/11/63 (22 + 11 = 33). Dealey Plaza is the site of the first Masonic temple in Dallas, and a Masonic obelisk. Why was it built there? The 33rd Parallel is of massive importance in occult sciences and Freemasonry. The rank of33$^{°}$ is the highest rank in Freemasonry you know. So, the following numbers all play a role, send out a message if you like; in the JFK assassination:

Number 11 -- November

Number 22 -- The day of the month

Number 33 -- Addition of '11' and '22'

Number 33 -- Dealey Plaza is located on the 33rd Parallel

You know all three of the 'George Bush's' are Freemasons I take it?'

'Yes.'

'But do you also know that they are all members of the Skull and Bones Society?'

'No, what's that?'

'It's a top secret society that believes in the power of occult practices.'

*

Thea Spiteri felt that there was still only one person on the island that she could trust. It was true that she didn't like his 'views' on certain things; particularly this 'Omerta' type oath that Corsicans seemed to adhere to; but she knew she could trust him to help rather than hinder, and that was all she asked. She drew up at Kevin Galea's front door a half hour later.

'Thea, what a lovely surprise, come in' said Kevin Galea; but Spiteri got the impression that it somehow wasn't a surprise. She wondered if the Commissioner had called Galea; warned him to expect a visit.

'Kevin, I'm sorry , but do you remember you once told me you wouldn't betray a fellow Corsican, but wouldn't stop me doing my job?'

'I do, yes.'

'Do you have a contact in the Corsican Police who has the same attitude?'

'I may have; this is about Sarti and Basti I take it?'

'You know?!'

'That depends on what you mean by "know".'

Spiteri decided to not even become involved in a discussion, as she knew from her previous discussions with Galea, and Tizian, that they viewed the world from a different perspective than others.

'Can you call him now, Kevin? I need to talk to him; it's important. Please.'

To her surprise, Galea did not leave the room to make the call. The call was answered and Spiteri picked up that Galea was calling someone called Marco. They had a brief chat and then Galea turned to Spiteri: 'he will answer what you ask…..no more, no less…..and only if he decides if it's relevant to your enquiry. Do you agree, Thea?'

'Yes.'

'She has agreed, Marco. I will leave the room now. Superintendent Spiteri will talk to you next; then, I'm sure, she will wish to go about her business.'

Galea handed Spiteri the phone: 'Let yourself out when you are finished, Thea.' Spiteri felt that she had just lost a friend.

Thea Spiteri had just started to give the stranger known as Marco some relevant background information when she was interrupted.

'Superintendent, I am aware of your interest; ask your questions.'

For fuck's sake; is there no end to this web?

'Who is Basti?'

'Was Superintendent, he's been dead many years; but, for the purposes of your enquiry; he was Nicola Tizian's father'

Spiteri closed her eyes: *this can't be happening.*

'Did he kill JFK?'

'I've no idea.'

'Did Sarti?'

'Again, I have no idea.'

'Do you know if he was ever in the USA?'

'Yes, he was.'

'Do you know anything about his life there?'

'Know anything? No. There were rumours of course, but.......'

'What kind of rumours?'

'The Corsican kind; murder, money and.....'

'And?'

'Love...... Superintendent. I understand you are experiencing that aspect of Corsica yourself at the moment.'

'And Basti experienced love in America?'

'There were rumours; yes.'

Spiteri.....her instinct kicking in ....'Did he have a child there?'

'There were rumours of an illegitimate son in the USA; yes. No-one really knew.'

'Do you know what this rumoured child's name was supposed to be?'

'Let me think: the name was something like......'

'Pietru Massa?'

'Quite so, Superintendent.'

Spiteri's visit left two people in a dilemma. Galea's dilemma was whether to do anything about what had just happened and, if he had to, he knew he had to move quickly. Spiteri's involved her heart. She called Nicola Tizian: 'Hi, will you be at home around 9.00 am tomorrow morning? I could pop in for breakfast; I'm going to be out that way anyway.'

'Great' replied Nicola Tizian.

The die was cast.

Chapter Twenty-Two

8.00 am
Tuesday
Spiteri's Home
'I have an appointment at 9.00 am Hunter. An appointment that actually has something to do with my priorities; you know; small things like three murders. It will take me half an hour to drive there, so I can't stand talking to you about, oh I don't know…..X Men, Hobbits, Spectre…..or any other nasty people. Sorry.'

'My, my Thea……I seem to have caught you at a bad time. Actually, I have an appointment shortly myself. You can collect your next, and final, envelope tonight......8.00 pm......I was so spoiled for choice for the location I must say....but finally decided on St Paul's Bay. Go down the steep road that takes you to Mellieha Beach. At the bottom, on the left, there is an old woman who sits there every evening selling pastizzi. She will give you the envelope.'

'How will she know me?'

'I told her to give it to the first harassed look-ing woman she sees!'

'Hunter.'

'Yes.'

'Fuck off.'

*

9.00 am

Tizian Villa

Nicola Tizian's Philippino maid opened the door to Spiteri in her usual off-hand manner. *She's in love with Nicola.....ergo.....hates me.*

Spiteri ignored the maid and walked into the main living room; her jacket draped over her arm.

'Darling; so good to see you, let me take your jacket.'

'Oh don't fuss, Nicola, it's OK here. I can't stay long anyway' said Spiteri, as she hung her jacket over the back of a chair.

'So to what do I owe the honour of your visit my darling?'

'Oh, nothing much really. What was it again? Ah yes, I remember now. Why did Pietru Massa kill Raymond Sarstedt, or if you prefer, Sarti? That would be the Pietru that you called Tony incidentally. And let's not forget the two Restins.'

'Pi, Pi….Pietru! He didn't!'

Spiteri tossed the CIA pic and artist impression sketch onto Tizian's marble coffee table.

'Nicola, I know Massa killed them all; I maybe can't prove it at the moment, but I know. That's three people he's killed, Nicola. Three people that he specifically came here to kill. Where is the gun he killed Sarstedt with, Nicola? The CIA are here; they're all over me… and asking about you. I need the truth, Nicola.'

Nicola Tizian's eyes appear to burn, his rage barely able to be controlled. Strangely, Spiteri did not feel fear, she was not afraid….but feared what was about to be said:

'OK Thea, you seem determined to destroy what we have; obviously, my love for you means nothing…..'

'That's just not true, Nicola. It's because I love you that I am here. If I didn't, other officers would be here; you know that, but if we are going to have any chance to be happy, then I need to know the truth.'

'Alright, I will tell you everything I know...... but I'll deny everything if you try to take it further. Will that satisfy you?'

'I don't know, Nicola, but......'

'Tizian raised his hand: 'I'll tell you what you want to know.....and finish up with a question for you. Can we agree on that at least?'

'OK.'

'....and you accept I'll deny this conversation ever took place?'

'Yes.'

Tizian paused, examined Spiteri.

'Undo your blouse.'

'What?'

'Oh, I think you heard me, Thea.'

'You think I'm trying to trap you, Nicola? Wearing a wire as your American associates might say? You think I would do that to you?'

'I don't know what to think about you now, Thea.'

Spiteri undid her blouse; turned full circle in front the man she was considering marrying, but there was no anticipation of pleasure to come on this occasion: 'Satisfied, Nicola?'

'Give me your phone and empty your hand-bag on the table.'

Spiteri did as he asked. Tizian glanced at the scattered contents as he removed the battery from Spiteri's phone: 'One can never be too careful, Princess.'

'Would that be the motto for our married life, Nicola?'

Tizian again stared deeply into Spiteri's eyes: 'Perhaps "Trust unconditionally" would be more suitable, Thea. What do you think?'

'Trust has to be won, Nicola.'

'Won? And tell me Superintendent, is that a two-way requirement?'

'Of course.'

'Then let's put that requirement to the test. Please, sit….this is a long story.'

*

Pietru Massa would have been more flattered than concerned had he known of the conversation taking place about him at that moment. The Boarding Gate at Malta International Airport for his flight to London had opened a few moments before and, as he strolled across the concourse to his flight; satisfied in what he had done for his family's honour, he heard neither the crack nor the screams.

Chapter Twenty-Three

'Nicola, before you start; I know a lot.....if your story waivers from the facts that I know; then I can't save you.'

'Pietru Massa is the illegitimate son of a man who was only known to me in stories as Basti.'

'Stories?'

'Corsican folklore, legends.....whatever.'

'OK.'

'Two or three weeks ago, a man I had never seen before walked into my life; and changed it forever. He told me he was Basti's son. He knew this because his mother was fiercely protective of him and wanted him to know all about his blood line. He had never known his father because he had returned to Corsica and settled there. That man was my father. Pietru Massa is my brother…..and he had come to Malta to save my life.'

'Who from?'

'Just listen, Thea. Pietru then told me a tale about our father that was so fantastical that I started to doubt his sanity. That was up until Sarstedt was killed.'

'The story being?'

'In short, a guy called Guestini hired my father, and another man named Sarti, to assassinate President Kennedy back in the '60's. My father returned to Corsica and settled down as the man I knew……or thought I knew. Years later, Sarti got in touch with him, in the 70's I think, my father was indebted to him in some way. Anyway, my father returned to the USA for a week or so; and he and Sarti killed Guestini. My father came home again….Sarti was eventually murdered himself. Story ends.'

'But obviously, it didn't end.'

'No. My brother runs a very successful Flying School business in the USA. One day this kid comes in for flying lessons. My brother takes to him, likes him, they became friends. But the young guy liked to brag, show off a little……you know how young people can be. The difference is that this guy liked to give the impression that he and his father were "connected." '

'As in Mafia?'

'Yea. Only he lets it slip one night that his father's real name is Guestini. Pietru doesn't know what to do, but in the end, he thinks "all the fathers are dead now....let it lie." But the two of them are at dinner one night and the guy is drunk and states that he and his father are flying out to Malta the following week to hook up with his mother; who's on a Mediterranean cruise with her sister – but really to "close my grandfather's account."

'To kill Hank Restin in other words?'

'Right. Pietru knows that Sarti's son; and his own half-brother; me, live in Malta. He puts two and two together and follows them out here. He finds me and tells me all this. Like I said, I'm stunned. Then Sarti Jnr is killed and we know it's true.'

'So you are saying that Hank Restin killed Sarstedt?'

'Yes.'

'And Pietru killed the Restin men?'

'I didn't say that.'

'Swear you played no active part in any of this, Nicola.'

'I swear. I never helped Pietru, Thea; I just never stopped him.'

Tizian and Spiteri's eyes both pleaded for understanding.

'Thea, we agreed I would finish with a question, did we not?'

'Yes.'

'So, here is my question: What is better in your view; that Guestini is dead, or that I am dead?'

'But what about Jon Restin?'

'Doesn't this story answer that question for you, Thea? A son will avenge his father, it is our way.'

'Jon Restin was an American, Nicola.'

'Yes, with Corsican blood in his veins. You asked, "What about Jon Restin"…I am merely giving you an answer as to why it happened; not giving it my approval. This way it is over.'

'Is it?'

'That is up to you now, Thea.'

'Where is Pietru now?'

'I honestly have no idea, Thea. He left; that is all I know.'

Spiteri studied the face of the man she had fallen in love with despite herself. She was an

experienced Pulizija Officer; she had interrogated
many people, she knew he was telling the truth.
Relief and happiness washed over her as she
walked into his outstretched arms.

As Nicola led her to the bedroom, Thea could
hear her mobile ringing: she gladly let it ring.

*

Thea Spiteri walked to her car in a state of
almost total happiness. Nicola had proved that he
was not complicit in any of the recent murders; if
not in his complete innocence of any knowledge
of them. But to the Corsican mind, that was
irrelevant. Spiteri dug her mobile from her bag as
she reached the car. She had several missed calls
from Mifsud and Said: *damn....but it was worth it.*

'Sorry, Raul, I've been tied-up. What's happening?'

'There's been a shooting at the airport. One
man is dead.'

'God, OK, I'll be there in 20 minutes. Any
details on the victim?'

'Not really......Only a name.'

'It's a start. Who is it?'

'An American.....a Mr Pietru Massa.'

Spiteri supported herself by leaning on her
car. 'Are you positive about that name?'

'Well, the face matches the passport. Why are
you asking; do you know him?'

'Make sure the scene is completely secured Raul; I'll be there as soon as possible.'

Nicola!.....what should I do?.....Mother of God, help me. No, I have to go to the scene; Nicola will find out soon enough.

Spiteri jumped into her car, but before she had moved her mobile rang. She considered ignoring it; then saw that it was the Commissioner.

'Yes, Commissioner.'

'Superintendent, come to my office straight away please.'

'Commissioner, I have just been informed of a murder at the airport. I'm on......'

'Superintendent, come to my office....now.'

The dialling tone let Spiteri know that the conversation was over.

*

The look on the faces of the two CIA men as she entered the Commissioner's office confirmed Spiteri's fears.

'One minute you ask about this guy Massa; next minute he's dead. He's a US citizen Superintendent, so before you go on the defensive, that makes this our business. What's the story?' Carter's rage was clear to see.

Despite her instinct to protect Maltese authority in the case; Spiteri knew that Carter was right. *Besides, nothing can be proved against Nicola.*

'Yes, I know, I understand. Pietru Massa did not kill……'

Carter's mobile went off: 'Shit, sorry….I have to take this. Carter….Jesus H Christ…..are you sure? OK, thanks.'

Carter stares over at Spiteri; his mind racing: 'Superintendent, you promised me that if there was any connection to my case, you'd tell me straight away.'

'I've only just found out about the connection! I was on my way here when I got a call telling me about the airport shooting……and that it was Massa who had been shot! What could I do?'

'So you made a connection before you found out that Massa was dead?'

'Yes.'

'And what connection would that be, Superintendent?'

Spiteri spends the next half an hour relating the whole story; as told to her by Tizian.

'Who put you onto the Massa connection?' asked Clark.

'I'm friends with the ex Pulizija Commission-er….Kevin Galea…..he got me access to a Corsican source.'

Carter and Clark exchanged glances.

'What?' asked Spiteri.

'Galea is a surname that's been floating about the JFK story for a while.'

'Oh for God's sake….do you people never use a bit of common sense? He was the Pulizija Commissioner here for Christ's sake!'

Carter nods to Clark and points to their private laptop: 'Check the Galea connection to the JFK / Corsican investigation. Do a background search on Kevin Galea; see if there's any link, no matter how tenuous.'

'Where does Galea live?' Carter asks Spiteri.

'Pembroke.'

An uneasy silence pervaded the room; no-one wished to speak, and Spiteri and Commissioner Malia were praying nothing would show up on the CIA search. Five minutes passed before a beep from the CIA laptop broke the silence.

'So, Galea's grandfather, one Frederico Galea, was married to one Aimee Guerini; sister of Antoine Guerini. The very same Antoine Guerini you just told us about, Superintendent.'

'That doesn't mean……'

'Thea, please…..it all fits. Galea is the shooter; he killed Sarti Jnr and Pietru Massa. Superintendent, no time for discussion, we must find that rifle. Get a team to meet us at Galea's house.'

'What?….what, are you talking about? This is madness!'

'Oh, didn't I say before; the bullet that killed Massa? It was fired from the Kennedy gun.'

Spiteri couldn't believe what she was hearing; the implications of what was being said.

'Thea…….I need to know……are you with us on this?'

Spiteri's sadness could only allow her to nod her agreement. *Please, God, he's not already on his way to Nicola.'*

Spiteri knew that she couldn't be directly involved in the arrest or interrogation of Kevin Galea; but she felt compelled to observe the proceedings from a distance if, for no other reason, than to check that her prayers have been answered and Galea was at home. On the way to Galea's house she had rung Nicola Tizian's mobile constantly; but got no response. Minutes seemed to drag by but finally she watched as the Galea's front door was opened, she sees a conversation taking place……and Kevin Galea being lead towards an unmarked car. *Thank God.*

*

Spiteri started her car and headed back to Nicola Tizian's home: *this will not be easy either, Thea.*

When Spiteri arrived at Tizian's home she knew that she wouldn't need to tell Nicola about his brother's killing. Black drapes were entwined around the front gates, and security men were everywhere to be seen.

She entered the kitchen; where Tizian was sitting with a bottle of Jack Daniels as his only company; Spiteri could see the anguish on his face.

'Thea, thank you for coming. Please....sit. Would you like a drink?'

'No, thank you. How are you?'

'Ha.....how am I? I am well......but my brother is not. Tell me what you know Thea; I will deal with the rest.'

'Nicola, I can't....sorry.'

'Sorry! You're fucking sorry! My brother is dead! Dead Thea....do you understand? Now, I say again, what do you know?'

'Nicola.....'

Tizian threw his glass against the far wall: 'I told you everything. You made love to me. Now my brother is dead and you won't help me!'

'I can't Nicola; I'm too scared about what you might do, and make more mistakes than you already have.'

'What do you mean....mistakes?'

'Hank Restin didn't kill Sarti.'

'What? Of course, he did!'

'He didn't.'

'How do you know this?'

'Because the gun that killed Pietru also killed Sarti.'

'Shit, Thea......that is not possible.'

'Nicola....it is true. We have made the link to Guerini, but it wasn't Hank Restin. Nicola, trust me.....we have already arrested this man and he will pay; but I can't give you his name. Sorry.'

Spiteri had expected an angry outburst from Tizian; but it was almost as if he had stopped listening to her....had retreated into his own world.

'Nicola, did you hear what I said?'

'What?.....I......'

'We have him; he will pay for Pietru's death.'

'OK.'

'Nicola, are you......'

'Thea, thank you for coming.....I'm sorry I shouted at you.....but I'd prefer to be alone now.'

*

Spiteri pulled into a lay-by about half a kilometre from Tizian's house; as her tears were making it hard for her to drive. *Oh Nicola, have I lost you now as well. Please, please don't do anything to spoil this chance we have.*

Spiteri dabbed her eyes with a tissue, applied some lipstick and looked in her rear view mirror: *you still have work to do Thea....so get on with it.* As if by summons; Spiteri's phone rang.

'Raul.'

'Superintendent, we have just been 'removed' from the Massa airport killing.......and informed in no uncertain terms that "it" had never happened.' Mifsud was shouting rather than speaking.

'Raul, I know it's difficult, but what I can tell you is that this killing is linked to the Sarstedt and Restin killings.....and the CIA have assumed control of the investigations. Take my word for it.....they're welcome.'

'But how......'

'Raul, it is what it is. Now leave it and move onto other cases.'

'Yes, Ma'am.'

Chapter Twenty-Four

Friday 24th

9.00 pm

Even though it was 9.00 pm, Kevin Galea was still sitting in a Pulizija Interview Room. One he had been in many times before; but the first time on this side of the table.

'Don't be ridiculous. You can search my home for the next 50 years and you will find no gun; especially a rifle you claim has recently killed two people…..and a former US President!'

'Galea, Spiteri told us everything. She came to you for help, and you certainly provided it!' said Clark.

'Correct; she came to me for help. I helped her. She is a friend; that is what friends do.'

'Yes, but helping in a crime, is a crime in itself; as I'm sure you're aware of......Ex-Commissioner.'

'Sneer if you like Gentlemen; it's an American trait I believe, but I have done nothing wrong. The opposite, in fact, I've probably saved lives.'

'How do you work that out?' said Carter.

'Well, at the last count, four people are dead, all Americans. The.....Ex-Commissioner in me, thinks this may be an American issue; not a Maltese one.'

'Clever Kevin; but no candy. Corsican blood is the link; and you, as it happens, are of Corsican extraction. Your Grandfather was married to the sister of one of the biggest criminals in the world, and we know that Sarti Snr and Basti Snr shot Kennedy. So if you think this is going away anytime soon, then you're mistaken.'

'In that case, I want my lawyer.'

Carter and Clark smiled at each other: 'Your lawyer? Forget that kind of crap Kevin. You'll be on a plane out of here, to destinations unknown, very shortly, if you don't start talking. Where did you go after Spiteri left your home?'

'Nowhere.'

'Nowhere? You'll need to do better than that.'

'It's true. I stayed in and read, you should try it sometime.'

'How do you know Hank Restin?'

'I don't.'

'Did you know Sarti Jnr; aka Sarstedt?'

'No.'

'Do you know Nicola Tizian?'

'Know of; yes.'

'What do you know?'

'He's a successful businessman on the island; he's been here many years.'

'From?'

'I'm sure you know.'

'Interesting don't you think?'

'Not particularly, no.'

'It's a pity for you that we do in that case.'

Carter and Clark rose from the table and walked to the room door.

'Get me my lawyer!'

Carter turned to Clark: 'Did you hear some-one speak just there?'

'No, can't say I did; must be the wind.'

*

9.05 pm

What is it people say: Thank God it's Friday. Well, Thea, today is Friday…..and it a complete bastard of a day.

Spiteri had just picked up the envelope from the 'pastizzi lady' in St Paul's and was heading home. Although she couldn't get thoughts of Kevin Galea's betrayal out of her head; she still found the whole scenario incomprehensible. *But Hunter is right Thea; you must find this fucking gun.*

By 10.00 pm Spiteri was sat in her home office, her trembling hands ready to open Hunter's latest revelations. *What is his interest in all this anyway, Thea? You need to pin him down more.* Spiteri was on her own as Helen had agreed, to Spiteri's surprise, to go to dinner with Jack Carter. *Then again, why not Thea…..nothing should surprise you anymore.*

Spiteri opened the envelope and laid the sheets out on her desk. *Well, here goes Thea.*

Sheet 1.
You may find this the most difficult information to absorb Superintendent; given the views of most Maltese people. I was going to get you to

spend time researching a lot of what is contained here, but I feel that time is running out, and so I have decided to lay the basic information, and allow you to assess it as you will.

We are agreed, I hope, that there were many groups with vested interests in seeing JFK gone. The last big player in that cabal was the Catholic Church.

Stop! I know what you are shouting even though I haven't called yet! "JFK was a Catholic, why would the Catholic Church want him dead?" Unpalatable to many it may be; but the reason is the same as all the others: power, money, greed.....being a big player in a new world order that ALL the groups in the cabal want to see happen.

You have asked me on many occasions: "what has this to do with Malta?" Let me explain.

I've shown you the proof of the involvement of Freemasonry in the assassination, and that symbolism is important to them. You have seen that many Jews are also Masons. It is clear that the CIA/FBI covered-up the truth. Now we come to the Catholic Church, or perhaps I should be more specific: The Knights of Malta.

In time, you can check out the following information in the Bibliotheca in Valletta; read what happened in Malta after WW 2.

OK, in Malta, Membership of the Freemasons is by invitation only. Candidates are required to be Master Masons, and Royal Arch Masons, and to sign a declaration that they profess the Doctrine of the Holy and Undivided Trinity.

The local bodies of the Knights of Malta are known as Priories; and they all operate under a Grand or Great Priory, often with an intermediate level of Provincial Priories.

Three degrees are administered in this system:
• The Degree of Knight Templar (Order of the Temple)
• The Degree of Knight of St. Paul (incorporating the Mediterranean Pass)
• The Degree of Knight of Malta (Order of Malta)

The Degree of Knight of Malta (Order of Malta) is universally associated with the Masonic Knights Templar. It is known by varying degrees of formality as the Order of Malta, or the Order of Knights of Malta, or the Ancient and Masonic Order of St John of Jerusalem, Palestine, Rhodes, and Malta. In practice, this last and fullest version of the name tends to be reserved for letterheads, rituals, and formal documents.

Thea, it is also important that you know of this bit of background to the Masonic code. There are two ranks that are the highest position a Mason can achieve and they are attained through the Templar Degrees in the Scottish Rite: the Accepted Scottish Rite of Freemasonry: the 32nd Degree (Master of the Royal Secret), and the 33rd Degree (Inspector General). The meritorious and highly symbolic 33rd degree, the Degree of the Illuminati, contains a three-word motto; 'Ordo Ab Chao.' This literally means 'From Out of Chaos Comes Order.'

I would think assassinating US President counts as "chaos." Therefore, if the elites can break down the existing order of society and the public cries out for the restoration of some semblance of this order, the elite will emerge as the true global rulers, and then, they will finally have the world that they so intensely desire. This 'new order' includes the subjugation of all levels of society subordinate to that of the Global Elite.

It is interesting to note is it not that Chief Justice of the Supreme Court, Earl Warren, was himself a 33rd degree Freemason, who was Grand Master of California from 1935 to 1936. His Warren Commission; all appointed by 33° Mason Lyndon Johnson, was filled with Freemasons. Gerald R. Ford, J. Edgar Hoover, and Allen Dulles were all 33° Freemasons as well.

Also interesting to note that Abraham Zapruder, of the famous "Zapruder film" himself, was a 32° Freemason, and after the assassination, he was raised to the 33°.

Last word on this issue, Thea, other high-level Freemasons directly involved in the murder of JFK included George Bush Sr., a 33° Freemason, as well as Bush Sr. belonged to Yale University's Skull and Bones occult society.

What is the link? Catholics [like Jews] cannot be Masons? Well the heads of the two most powerful Jewish families in the world; The Rothschild's and the Rockefeller's are Freemasons; and one of the strongest Lodges is called P2; and is based in the Vatican. J Edgar Hoover, G W Bush Jnr, Cartha DeLoach [FBI No 3 behind Hoover] were, or still are, Knights of Malta. Finally, if you think that this is all in the past: in 2004 5 Masonic Lodges were instituted in Malta. A further Lodge; "The White Sea Lodge", was founded in 2010, followed by the "Mare Nostrum Lodge" in 2011…..taking the total to 9.

***

As if fate were playing a role; Spiteri's mobile rang. 'Please don't tell me Al Pacino's involved somehow……………'

'It's hard to take in, I realise that.'

'I'm not sure I want to take it in; ignorance is bliss and so-on.'

'But at least now you see the importance of the gun, and why so many people want it.'

'Including you, Hunter.'

'That's true Thea, but I am the only one who has tried to help you.'

'What now?'

'I can do very little more. I will keep in touch. Good luck in your quest.'

….and so to bed…..tomorrow is another day.

Chapter Twenty-Five

Saturday

Despite; or maybe because of, everything, Spiteri had managed to sleep for a solid 10 hours. When she eventually wandered into the kitchen, Helen had coffee and pancakes ready and waiting: 'I heard that you were up. Rough night?' asked Restin.

'No, not at all, just worn out I think. This whole CIA involvement is a real pain. Oh sorry, Helen…how did your date go?'

'Date! I hope you're not being serious. I just felt like a change of scenery, someone else to talk to. No offence though Thea, you have been marvellous.'

'Oh none was taken; I understand. Are you looking forward to going home on Monday?'

'....yes.'

Spiteri thought she detected doubt in Restin's reply. 'Do you want to do anything, in particular, this weekend?'

'Aren't you busy?'

'I have some work to do but its paperwork; I can do it at home anytime.'

'Are you any closer to closing your cases?'

'Not really. Did Carter mention anything?'

'No, I told him when we made the arrangements that there was to be strictly no shop talk.'

'Good move.'

'OK; let's get dressed, go out for a drive and get some lunch. We can maybe watch a movie tonight?'

'Sounds perfect.....and thank you again, Thea.....I don't know how I would have gotten through this without you. I think you saved my life; maybe I'll return the favour one day.'

'You just buy the lunch and we'll leave it at that.'

Saturday seemed to pass in the blink of an eye for both Helen and Thea. They had forgone the movie idea and contented themselves sharing a bottle of wine and watching the evening turn into night. Sunday followed in a similar vein up until about 8.00 pm when Helen asked if Thea minded if she went to bed early: 'long day ahead tomorrow.' Spiteri was happy to agree as it would give her the time to try and get down on paper the various thoughts….and questions…..that had been swirling in her head since her last conversation with Hunter on Friday. She 'retired' to her office: *right here goes.*

What do I know for sure?

JFK and Raymond Sarstedt / son of assassin Sarti - both killed with the same gun.

Gun must be in Malta [or was?]

JFK shooter; Basti, is Nicola's father and father of US businessman, P Massa

Massa shot dead

Probably know?

Hank [& son, Jon] Restin [Guerini] came here to kill Sarti & Nicola.

The R's didn't succeed though as Massa killed by the same gun and Restins already dead by that point.

Massa [N's half-brother] found out about the plan and killed both Restins [before he too was killed] He wasn't even on Malta when Sarti was killed so he's not the killer. Could it have been Nicola???????

Questions

Has the gun been on Malta since 1964?
Someone knew where it was and how to access it.
They got the gun.....killed Sarti. Why?
They killed Massa. Why?
They didn't kill N. Why not?
Is the gun still on the island?

Conclusions

Finding the gun will maybe explain WHY everybody wants it.....but WON'T necessarily show me who my killer is.

Nicola arranged all 4 killings. Why? Would he kill his own brother?

If not Nicola; who 'needed' Sarti and Massa dead? Why? CIA????

<u>Answers</u>
<u>NO FUCKING IDEA</u>
Shit.

Spiteri's mobile danced across the table; the blank screen indicating only one thing.

'Is it true that someone else has been killed by the gun?' This was the first time Spiteri had sensed anxiety in Hunter's voice.

'Yes.'

'You need to find the gun!'

'No Hunter I don't. Finding the gun may be of great importance to some people but not me. I've gone along with your project and, yes, I've had my eyes opened and yes, I now know that powerful people cross over all the different fraternal, religious organisations and secret societies in order to achieve their goals. Tough, but I can't solve the problems of humanity; nor can I solve a 50-year-old crime. I'm sorry, but all I want is to find out who killed Raymond Sarstedt and Pietru Massa and bring him to justice. To be honest; I don't really care what his reasons were, what secret fucking groups he was in or whether God is Catholic, a Freemason, a Jew, a shareholder in the Federal Reserve Bank or Batman's cousin.'

'I understand that Thea, but to find your killer you will need to find the gun. Ours is a symbiotic relationship; a mutual need.'

'Ah, I'm glad you've brought that point up. Who are you working for; why do you want the gun? Which group of wankers do you represent I wonder?'

'You're tired Thea; get some sleep.'

'You're right Hunter, I am tired.....tired of you.'

*

Spiteri lay on the top of her bed. Her anger at Hunter was gone but she was less than elated at how it was possible to have four murders on her island, and she had no control over what was being done to solve them. Everyone only cared about finding the gun.

Why? Even if someone had the gun in their hand right now; today....so what? At the end of the day, it's just a gun. OK, historic interest....it's not as if the bloody thing can speak. Kevin Galea too; what possessed him? Anyway, sleep, see Helen off tomorrow then see how things go.

Spiteri had considered not telling Helen Restin of the new developments surrounding the deaths of her husband and son, but knew that she had to. Spiteri also felt that she may have to say to Helen Restin that she could no longer leave the island; *she's a possible suspect, Thea, she could have "hired" Massa*...but she decided to put that particular decision off until she had more details of what the circumstances surrounding the two deaths were. *You don't know yet for sure that these are murders, Thea. Besides, yes, a woman may well kill her husband....but her son as well?*

Chapter Twenty-Six

Monday 25th Jan

The following morning; when Helen Restin realised that Spiteri was going to the Pulizija station in St Julians that day; she suggested that she drop her off as she was returning the Hire Car there anyway.

On the way there, Restin appeared wistful.

'You won't miss this place I imagine, Helen?'

'Strangely, I think I will. It's true Thea; there is something about this island. I think I could live here one day.'

'You might find it a bit dull, Helen!'

'Perhaps, but maybe dull is another word for "no drama" '

Spiteri's phone rang: 'Hi, Nicola.'

'Good morning, Princess. I' m so sorry for yesterday, I was feeling overwhelmed. I'd like to speak to you about Pietru's body; where are you?'

'I'm driving along on this lovely sunny day; just entering St Julians.'

'Your own car, or are you being chauffeured around by a handsome young Constable to try and make me jealous?'

'Neither, I'm with Helen. She's dropping me at the station in St Julians....then taking her hire car back to the Hilton. Then she's heading to the airport; she leaves today.'

'Helen..........Helen who?'

'Helen Restin, I told you, she stayed with me over the holidays.'

'You didn't say her actual name, Thea. Are you far from Avis?'

'No, practically there. I'm just about to jump out and walk actually; let Helen turn up to the hotel.'

'Thea.......'

'What?'

'Nothing.'

'Hello, Nicola, hello......

Spiteri looked over at Helen with a shrug of the shoulders: 'Lost the signal!......Helen, just drop me here at this mini-roundabout.....I'll walk down to the station, it's just at the bottom of the hill.....and you're only a minute from the Hilton here. Have a safe journey, and let me know once you are home.'

Spiteri was sad to see her friend go but felt sure they would meet again. She strolled down the hill, enjoying the sun and the slight breeze blowing in from St Julians Bay and skipped up the stairs leading into the Pulizija Station. She was just about to say hello to the two officers manning the Reception area; when she was surprised by the sound of distant thunder.

Well, that's a surprise; it's such a lovely day.

Spiteri glanced over to the two officers again.... when she was stopped in her tracks by the sound of breaking glass.....and screaming; lots of screaming.

Spiteri raced to the front door of the station; closely followed by the two on-duty Constables. A river of people was flowing down the hill to the left of the station; away from a large plume of black smoke that had appeared, from Spiteri's point of vision, above a "Diamonds International" complex that sat opposite the Portomaso Marina.

'Gas explosion; gas explosion!' one fleeing woman shouted to the two Pulizija officers. Both were already on their radios and running up the hill against the tide of humanity coming in the opposite direction.

Two other Pulizija officers crashed through the station doors, trying to assess the situation.

Spiteri shouted over: 'Gas explosion…..make sure all the Emergency Services are on their way.' She herself was in a quandary as to whether to race to the scene or keep out of the way and let the professionals get on with it. The sound of numerous sirens wailing their way to the scene convinced Spiteri just to go back home: *nothing worthwhile for you to do, Thea….go home…..you'll be busy enough.*

Spiteri collected a pool car from behind the station and headed home. The house seemed deserted now; she was missing Helen already. Spiteri made herself a coffee and drank it while flicking through an old copy of The Malta Times. The term "News Update" caught her eye: *what are you doing looking at old news Thea….put the TV on…..see what's happening with the gas explosion.* She settled on her couch and pressed the 'On' button on her remote. Unknown to her Nicola Tizian was doing exactly the same thing.

"Go News Update: "The woman driver of what is believed to be a hired car has been killed in what Pulizija are saying appears to be a bomb blast. However, they are stressing that there are no indications that there are any terrorism concerns surrounding the bombing. The blast occurred outside the Portomaso Hilton; where the car hire company, Avis, have an office."

Spiteri's brain took a few seconds to take in the report: *What....but....a bomb......what car...maybe if....*

Robot- like Spiteri walked back into her kitchen: *Please God, not Helen, don't let it be her.....*

But Spiteri knew it was; had to be. Her mind was racing. She knew there was nothing she could do that wasn't already being done: *Well perhaps one last thing, Thea.* She picked up her phone and called the Commissioner; she was put through immediately.

'The woman who was killed in the bomb blast......I'm sure it's Helen Restin.'

'Good God.'

'I know.....one trip to Malta, and three members of a family wiped out. I can't be in-volved in the investigation obviously, we were friends, she had been staying with me, but I'm probably the only person who will be able to identify the body. Has she been taken to the morgue?'

'Thea, she has but……'

Spiteri's heart missed a beat: 'but what…..is it not her?'

'No…it's just that there isn't really a body to identify. Sorry. We'll get her identified through DNA…..we're already on it; Carter's pulling strings Stateside.'

'Right, thank you. Tell Carter I'm at home please; he'll want to talk to me I'm sure, but I can't face driving there. Sorry.'

'That's quite alright, Superintendent….I understand. I'll see you tomorrow, and Carter can wait till then I'm sure'

'Thank you, Commissioner. Goodbye.'

'Superintendent, one last thing; an order if you will.'

'Yes?'

'Don't go to the morgue.'

Spiteri trudged back into her kitchen, threw the remains of her coffee into the sink, and opened a bottle of wine. *What, how, why…..none of this makes sense.* Spiteri's head began to pound; she made her way into her bedroom and lay down.

The Maltese Hunter

She was asleep in seconds; the nightmares would take longer to come.

Chapter Twenty-Seven

Tuesday

Kevin Galea would not have believed that what was happening to him was possible; not in a 'civilised' society. He had been left sitting in a darkened room for endless hours. He had been allowed no phone calls and no visitors. *If they can do this to me; what can they do to less powerful people? And who exactly are "they." Perhaps they are not CIA at all.* When he heard the key rattle into the lock of the room, Kevin Galea had no idea if he was being released, questioned further…..or would be boarding a plane to a European "Guantanamo Bay."

*

Thea Spiteri knew she had to carry-on; but didn't feel as though she could.

Her friend Helen was dead. Her friend Kevin was a killer. Her friend Miriam was a killer. Her boyfriend was probably a killer…..and she'd just found out that someone who had haunted her thoughts for over twenty odd years; Red O'Toole, had killed himself, and would no doubt haunt her for another twenty years now. *Focus Thea….focus.* Spiteri had accepted that the things that 'Hunter' had said were compelling, and she resolved to look at the JFK case as one of her own as he had suggested, but *even if I solve it, so what, why is finding this gun so important? Right Thea…..Motive – Means – Opportunity….let's get started….give it a couple of days….then that's it.*

Spiteri had been granted two days off because of Helen Restin's death but was glad to busy herself by focusing on other things. Over many long hours, Spiteri studied the pointers that 'Hunter' had mentioned; did her own research; cross-referenced everything she could….and came up with three lists, and two conclusions;

one of which troubled her more than a little. *Just what exactly are you caught up in here, Thea?*

1 - The Means: Just who could pull off this crime?

This crime required money, expert planning, the authority to "set-up" the scene and aftermath…..and expert marksmen…..something that Lee Harvey Oswald was not.

Spiteri had decided at the beginning to "plan" an assassination of the Maltese Prime Minister to try and get an idea of what would need to be covered in order to achieve A. The killing B. Someone to blame. C. A manipulated investigation D. The money to pay the shooters. E. The power to suppress further investigation. It hadn't taken her long to realise that even a vastly scaled-down operation in Malta, compared to what would be required in the USA, would require significant numbers of powerful people to be involved.

The "Lone Gunman" theory was absurd. Over 100 witnesses near the "grassy knoll" reported hearing…Bang…pause…bang, bang in a rapid sequence. Three salvos, nine shots…..a sequence of firing that isn't even possible using the kind of bolt action rifle the investigation said was used. Even the 'famous' backyard pictures of Oswald holding the supposed murder weapon, show a different rifle to the one they later said fired the shots. Is this why Carter is here?

The final "powerful people" proof was the death of Oswald himself. *What police force in the world would have a prisoner that had supposedly just committed the "crime of the century".....yet would allow a known criminal stroll into the station, armed; and shoot the suspect!*

Furthermore, one of the Police Officers in the hall at the time stated that they had received "instructions" that Oswald had to be handcuffed "spread eagle style" to two officers [instead of the usual one] when being taken to Court. This then prevented Oswald from bringing an arm up to protect himself when Jack Ruby approached him.

2. Motive – who wanted the victim dead

There's not enough paper on Malta to list the number of people who seemed to want Kennedy out of the way.

Spiteri found ample evidence to support the arguments involving Johnson, CIA, FBI, rich oil men, bankers, the Mob.....but had to admit to herself that she had been unaware that, at the time, Israel wanted to have nuclear capability, and that Kennedy was fiercely opposed to it. *Could there be a link there, Thea? God knows, the world is a terrible place. And what is the link to Malta?*

3. Opportunity

No denying Oswald had the opportunity, Thea. That's true, but you have to look deeper. It wasn't Oswald, alone, who 'manufactured' the opportunity. Oswald didn't call off the normal security arrangements surrounding a President. Oswald didn't turn the car onto Elm St at such a snail's pace and then stop the car when the firing started, instead of speeding off. Oswald didn't issue the order that no Secret Service men had to stand on the limo's running boards, as was the usual procedure. Finally, in a Presidential motorcade, a Press and film flatbed truck are always at the front, recording the events for posterity. It wasn't Oswald who told the driver of the truck that he wasn't to go at the front this time.

This was a set-up, Thea. That's a certainty…. but what is so important about this fucking rifle; especially after all this time. Jesus. Only one way to find out…………..speak to Jack Carter……and find out why he lied to me about Sarti while I'm at it.

*

'Jack, it's Thea.'
'Hi….sorry to hear about Helen, I gather you had become friends.'

'Thanks. The DNA in from the US yet?'

'No, it will be here tomorrow, though.

'That's good. Anyway, Jack, do you like Maltese wines?'

'Well, I can't say I've tasted that many to say.'

'OK, get directions to my house and come over this afternoon about 3.00 pm. I'll educate you!'

'I know where you live.'

'Yes, I suppose you do Mr Bond.'

'See you at 3.00.'

Gently does it, Thea, gently does it.

It was about 3.30 pm when Jack Carter realised that he could forget any notion of romance that had somehow entered his head after Spiteri's earlier invite.

'Who would you say is the most important person in the world, Jack?'

'The President of USA.'

'Any particular one; or the Post in general?'

'The post.'

'What if you thought your President was really wrong about a lot of things? You felt he was making decisions that were going to cost American lives?'

'That's not for me to decide.'

'What if one, or more, of your superior officers in the CIA approached you about getting rid of a President…..a President that you personally couldn't stand anyway?'

'Getting rid of?'

'Assassinating.'

'Could never happen.'

'Really? Have you ever heard of someone called E Howard Hunt, Jack?'

'What's all this about, Superintendent?'

'Why did you tell me Lucien Sarti died in a French brothel?'

'He did.'

'Really? Well, I've been having a look at a lot of things surrounding the JFK killing.'

'And?'

'And…..Lucien Sarti was, apparently, killed in Mexico in 1972. It wasn't reported at all in the American press; funny that.'

'He was a 'nobody'; why report it?'

'Why lie? And in Mexico City too; what a co-incidence!'

'Why's that?'

'Oh, it's just that the guy Hunt I mentioned; the one you don't seem to have heard of, even though he was Head of the CIA, and he headed up your operations in Mexico City at one time.'

'Not in 1972.'

'No, you're quite right about that. It was in 1963…..the time that Lee Harvey Oswald; the man who you yourself say was framed for the JFK assassination, was there. Oops, another coincidence!'

'There's no evidence they ever met.'

'That's true. There's no evidence he met Sarti there either, but that doesn't mean he didn't. Have you ever heard of 3 guys called; Meyer, Harvey and Morales.'

'No.'

'Thought not…..it's just that they were the three former CIA operatives that Hunt mentioned in his death-bed confession; said they helped him in the Kennedy assassination.'

'Aliens from outer space have been mentioned too.'

'True, but I think little green men would have been spotted on the grassy knoll, don't you? That's not to say the CIA wouldn't have been able to cover it up mind you. A bit like Alpha 66, or have you not heard of them either, Jack?'

'Look……'

'No, you look, Carter. You've appeared from nowhere into my country, rode roughshod over my jurisdiction and, worst of all, asked for my help while keeping secrets.'

'I ……..'

'Shut up. Don't panic, I haven't solved your crime of the century for you. All I want from you is the truth about two things.'

'Which are?'

'This rifle you're so keen to get a hold of; what is so special about it? Who was, or should that be is, Alpha 66? Are you one of them?'

'That's three things.'

'Let's make it four then: do you want my help or not?'

Carter got up from his kitchen stool and walked over to the glass, patio doors. 'Lovely home.'

'Thanks.'

'Alpha 66 was a clandestine group of CIA operatives who took "missions" upon themselves; missions that they had no "official" approval for. Missions that they themselves deemed necessary.'

'Including murders?'

'Yes.'

'Hence things like the Bay of Pigs?'

'Yes.'

'But if these things weren't official, who paid for them?'

'In that case, Santo Trafficante and other Mobsters; they were desperate to get the Havana casinos and drug businesses back.'

'Nice. Does it still exist?'

'I honestly don't know, Thea. I do know that I am not a member if that is what you are really asking.'

Spiteri studied Carter: 'I believe you.'

'Thank you. Do you know where the rifle is, Thea?'

'No…..I think only Kevin will know that.'

'I believe you.'

'What now?'

'I'll wait to be told. I expect we'll be told to go back home.'

'And Kevin…..I can't allow you to take him. Any trial will be here.'

'That's out of my hands, Thea. Your Prime Minister and my President will decide I suppose.'

'Yes, I suppose they will.'

Chapter Twenty-Eight

Wednesday

Spiteri slept the same troubled sleep she had been experiencing the last few nights. She knew from experience that this kind of thing just happened to her when there were things not making sense to her in her investigations; even if the doubts were in her subconscious somewhere. *You just have to let them come through, Thea.....they always do.*

The following morning, Spiteri was tired and in no mood to think any more about assassinations or missing men. She spoke to Sarah Said briefly for any updates, but there was nothing new of major importance. The gentle thud of the post being delivered would change that.

Amongst the bills and junk, one letter stood out. The address was hand-written and the envelope had been hand delivered. Spiteri opened her door and looked around but didn't see anyone, not even the Malta Mail delivery person.

Spiteri wandered back into her kitchen, threw the regular mail into a wicker fruit bowl that sat on a worktop, and opened the hand delivered letter. But it wasn't a letter or even a note; it was a photograph......a photograph of a rifle. Spiteri had never seen the rifle before, but she knew what it was. Slightly dazed by the impact that the photo had made on her, Spiteri poured herself another coffee and took it and the picture into her home office. Once seated, and with hands that had only just stopped shaking, Spiteri pulled over a pen and pad and started a list of every little thing she could remember that she had picked up in conversations; but not yet acted upon.

She scribbled "Hunter" on the first page, then a numerical list below.

Antoine Guerini......why was he picked?

Trafficante....."order from elsewhere." Who???

The Cabal.....but who proposed it???

Who shot Oswald – real name – Jewish – so what? - any significance

Who got Oswald the job in the Book Depository, only 1 week before the Kennedy schedule had been changed by LB Johnson? Find this out !!!!

Immigrants are always changing their names.... "to fit in"....*or disguise their origins??*

Find the gun.....find your killer??? Why has Hunter kept saying that????

Carter:

Admitted that Oswald was innocent..."a patsy"......the 'accepted' story for 50 years, though.....so why still so keen on finding the real rifle now?

Lied about Sarti.

Names......Corleone?......Basti?.....Galea?...... Sarstedt? What if.............

Nicola:

Named "wealthy Jews" amongst the many suspects. So did Hunter, but not Carter. Why?

OK, Thea…..one by one.

Less than an hour had passed; Spiteri reviewed her notes:

Antoine Guerini…..the Mob picked him…..so the order never came <u>from</u> him.
Trafficante's lawyer admits that…..the Mob didn't issue the order…..but were willing to be told what to do……So; Powerful people……who????
Bankers…the paymaster…..Rockefeller and Rothschild families: Jew / Israel

She needed to see someone's reaction face to face to help her know what was real.
Thea, this is all interesting, frightening even, but it's still nothing new….it's not proof of anything.

Spiteri picked up the picture again. This time, she noticed a rectangular mark on the butt. She had thought it was just the manufacturer's mark, but decided to take a closer look with a magnifying glass:
"To my brother Antoine: with much love. D G."
She picked up her phone and called Jack Carter and half an hour later, Spiteri was sitting in

her office, opposite a rather nervous looking Jack Carter.

'I need to thank you for something, Jack.'

'Oh, what would that be?'

'For pointing out the peculiarity of names.'

'Sorry?'

'Names, Jack…people's names…..they change. Your Mum probably called you John.'

'I don't see…..

'Then let me enlighten you. We all agree that Oswald was a diversion. We all also agree that no single group organised the assassination of Kennedy.'

'OK, and……'

'And? What we still don't know is who was at the very pinnacle of the pyramid; who started the ball rolling, and that, Jack, is why you are so desperate to find the gun. What I can't decide though is whether you know, and want it kept quiet, or you don't know, but feel the gun can tell you in some way.'

'All very interesting Superintendent; but what has any of this got to do with names?'

'Everything Jack; everything. I've been doing my own research, Jack. Who killed Oswald, Jack? You said yourself Oswald was set up to be the "patsy." But you forgot to mention his link to a company called Permindex which was a Mossad front organisation and our friendly CIA agent E. Howard Hunt who wanted the assassination attempt to implicate Cuba. You were also telling the truth when you said that the real assassins were French Corsicans; but, once again, you forgot to mention that Yitzhak Shamir; a Mossad assassin himself, was involved. The fatal shots were then fired from the 'Grassy Knoll' by Sarti and probably one or two others. Oswald was arrested and charged with 2 murders. Enter Jack Ruby to seal the plot.'

'There you go, Jack Ruby…..he's the guy that killed Oswald; you've just said it yourself!'

'Correct……and his real name was?'

Spiteri could see the blood drain from Carter's face: 'that's got…….'

'Rubenstein.'

'So what?'

'Let me ask you another.'

'Who got Oswald the job in the Texas Book Depository? A job incidentally that was never advertised but that an Application Form supposedly written by Oswald, mysteriously appeared after the shooting.'

'No-one knows for……..'

'Crap Jack. <u>George de Mohrenschildt</u>, who worked for Jewish oil barons, and who had connections to the CIA, got his friend, a Mrs

Paine, who worked in the personnel department there at the time, to give Oswald a job......any job. Why was that do you think, Jack?'

'That still......'

'This plot needed lots of money Jack; who supplied that? The Federal Reserve by any chance; which, as you no doubt know is owned by Rothschild and Rockefeller; and a Swiss bank, owned by top Jewish gangster, Meyer Lansky.'

'OK, so some rich & powerful Jews in America wanted JFK out, there was a danger of him affecting their wealth, but you said yourself there were numerous groups involved!'

'True; but what head, of which group, pressed the Go button, Jack? Which brings me back to your desperation to get the gun. Is it special, Jack......is it a talking rifle?' Spiteri studied Carter's body language intensely.

'In a way, it might be.'

'What do you mean?'

'Since Day 1, there has been a rumour that the rifle has a damning inscription on it.'

'Damning in what way?'

'No-one is sure' said Carter, as he shuffled a pen about on Spiteri's desk.

'Really.....an inscription like this do you mean?' said Spiteri as she threw down the picture of the rifle, and the brass plate: 'I'm guessing the Antoine is your Antoine Guerini; am I right?'

'Who knows?'

'I do.'

'Look, Superintendent of this tiny shit-hole; where is the gun, do you have it?'

'Jack, Jack…..I'm not finished talking about names. As you know, immigrants change their names a lot of the time. I checked up on Mr Guerini. His real name was Guerin, but I suspect you already knew that. Once I knew that too; it wasn't too much of a stretch to link Guerin to the DBG on the rifle. But who could it be Jack; what a puzzle eh?'

Carter sat ashen-faced; but Spiteri felt no sympathy for him.

'So, back I go to Antoine. Born in Po-land……any information on other family members I wonder. Not much, just that his father was called Victor……and, oh yes, a brother called…David. Gosh, that was a coincidence eh Jack? I'll take a look….see if David Guerin has a mention anywhere. No! No way, Jack….can it be true? My, my….there he is…David Ben Guerin…..who changed his name to….David Ben-Gurion….and ended up as Prime Minister of Israel in 1963. Mm, 1963…..wasn't that the year your President was gunned down, Jack?'

'Look, if…….'

'The JFK killing was a political assassination ordered by Israel wasn't it? The same Israel that the good old boys of the USA support so strongly now?'

Carter jumped to his feet: 'Fucking bitch…..Where did you get that picture…..where is the rifle?'

'Carter, I honestly don't know; but if I ever find out, you'll be the last to know. Now you and your pal with the matching Masonic rings;………… get off my island.'

Back in the quiet of her own home, Spiteri was still reeling from the events of her day. Her phone rang.

'Princess, how would you like to be treated to dinner?'

'Oh Nicola, that would have been lovely, but I've had a stressful day and just need to sleep. How about tomorrow?'

'Of course……lunch by my pool, say around 1.00 pm?'

'Perfect…..good night, Nicola.'

It would be anything but a good night for Spiteri though.

Chapter Twenty-Nine

Jumbled visions and words had started to haunt Spiteri. Her mind was trying to work out a solution for her, but key points were missing.

No, you're wrong that's not right….car…..Hunter…...walk…...Carter…you bitch….DBG…two DBGs. Spiteri woke with a start, unable to fathom where she was for a moment. *I'll call Nicola, ask him to come over. No, don't do that Thea….you want to be alone….a Greta Garbo night. Nicola…......call?*

Spiteri rose from her bed slowly. She went into her en-suite bathroom and splashed cold water on her face; peering at the mirror as she dried off......wondering who the woman staring back really was. She couldn't really say for sure, but she did know the truth about the killings.

She moved quickly to the hall, picked up her car keys....and sped off. Twenty minutes later, she walked into the hostel where Jafar was staying with other refugees. The Hostel Manager informed her that Jafar was no longer there: 'he managed to get a job I think.'

'Do you know where?'

'Sorry, no.'

Spiteri's frustration showed on her face as she turned and started to leave the hostel.

'Excuse me, I did see him going into the "Juliani" Hotel in St Julians the other day; he's maybe working in the kitchens there, but I don't know for sure.'

'Thank you, I'll check there.'

Ten minutes later, Spiteri approached the Receptionist in the Juliani Hotel. She discreetly showed her I.D. and was impressed that the receptionist didn't become agitated by an unexpected visit by the Pulizija; as many people do.

'I'm looking to see if a man; Jafar Nimeiri is an employee her?'

'No, I don't think so, but hold on & I will check.' The receptionist was off the phone in a few seconds.

'No, we have no-one of that name working here.'

'That's OK, I wasn't sure.'

'The name does sound familiar, hold on.' The receptionist went on to her computer. 'Yes, I thought so. Mr Nimeiri is a guest here.'

Spiteri kept her surprise to herself. 'Can you tell me his room number please?'

'Let me see: Room 23. The second floor, on the left as you come out of the lift.'

'Thank you……please do not call him.'

Spiteri ignored the lifts and walked up to the second floor: 'It's all beginning to make sense; but…..'

She knocked on the door of Room 23.

*

Jack Carter paced the Commissioner's office: 'You are her commanding officer for fuck's sake; a 32° Grand Master, a Knight of Malta and you're telling me you can't interfere in her investigation?'

'There's no need, she will not find the gun.'

'You said that at the start…..now you've lost the fucking thing!'

'It is not lost, merely displaced. It will be returned to safe keeping.'

'It fucking better be.'

*

The door to Room 23 opened slowly.

'Hello Jafar….or should I say Hunter?'

'Well done, Thea…….come in…..I knew you would get there in the end' said Jafar, in perfect English.

'What are you really doing here Jafar; which one of the Groups has hired you?'

Jafar smiled: 'It's a long, but simple story, Thea. I'm a Palestinian. We have always believed that Israel was behind the Kennedy shooting, we knew about the inscription on the gun. Like Mossad, we have many ears and eyes, we monitor the Jewish controlled CIA, and so we came here.'

'But why did you risk your life coming into the country the way you did?'

'Authenticity……I wanted to be one of the many…..to be invisible, but in fairness I was always safe although it had its moments!'

'Was it you that sent me the picture?'

'Picture?'

'Of the gun.'

'No. Do you have the gun?'

'No.'

'So you know who does have it?'

'No, the picture was delivered anonymously.'

'Can I see it?'

'No.'

'Why not?'

'I'm scared what you might do; that the picture would be enough for you.'

'Thea, even if I had the gun, never mind a picture, I would do nothing with it.'

'I don't understand. I would have thought that you would want the truth to come out as soon as possible?'

'Thea, this dispute has lasted over two thousand years; there is no hurry. But if the CIA get the gun then the truth will be lost forever. We have to wait until the US will be more 'receptive' to the truth. Also, at the moment, Palestine has its own internal political battles going on. Once we see who succeeds Abbas....then we will decide '

*

Spiteri left the hotel and went to her car. She sat for ten minutes before starting off on what she knew was going to be a fateful journey; she drove slowly, wracked her brain for an alternative, but knew there was none. Ten minutes later she arrived. She strode through Nicola Tizian's mansion doors without ringing for any sour faced Philippino to announce her.

'Hello, Nicola.'

Nicola Tizian swirled around in his seat: 'Thea, darling, so great to see you. I wasn't expecting you till much later.'

'Great?.............Don't you mean surprising?'

'What do you mean?'

'How did you know Helen Restin had hired her car from Avis, Nicola?'

'What?......I'm not sure what you mean; you told me yourself! Would you like a drink, Princess?'

Nicola Tizian walked over to his drinks cabinet and stretched under the counter for a glass; before slowly turning towards Spiteri. He had no drink in his hand; only a Beretta.

His face showed no emotion as he saw the gun in Spiteri's hand.

'You worked out it was Helen Restin who was the shooter; didn't you, Nicola. She killed Pietru and Sarstedt…..and you and Pietru killed two innocent men. So, when we were busying ourselves interrogating Kevin Galea; you were busy putting a bomb in Helen's car.

'Thea, I'll ask you again. The Restins were here to kill me. Would you have preferred that? We can still make this work.'

'You were willing to let me die in that car, Nicola. There is no "this." '

Thea Spiteri and Nicola Tizian's eyes searched each other's faces; both looking for answers to so many questions. Could any of them see love in the other? Nicola Tizian saw regret...and doubt. Thea Spiteri saw betrayal......and emptiness.

Neither of the former lovers was aware of either time nor place; all was silence.......

.......till two shots rang out.

THE END

Epilogue

The next day
"<u>Go News</u> – Pulizija have now identified and named the woman killed in the bomb blast outside the Portomaso Hilton as; Connie Farrugia, the Manageress of the Avis Car Rental outlet attached to the hotel."

*

Two days later
When Thea Spiteri opened her eyes, she saw a bright light, unfamiliar walls and a man in a white coat.

'You're in Mater Dei, Thea…..you're going to be alright.' Spiteri turned to see the smiling face of Kevin Galea.

'Nicola?'

'Nicola is dead, Thea.'

Even closing her eyes tightly could not prevent the tears from cascading down Spiteri's cheeks.

The words: 'I killed him' barely audible as she buried her face in her pillow.

'No, Thea, you didn't.'

Spiteri lay perfectly still: 'What do you mean?'

'Your gun jammed; you never fired a shot.'

'Then how……..'

'Nicola was shot from a distance.'

'What do you mean: "From a distance"? '

'Not by someone in the room; and there's more, he was killed by the JFK gun. That is why I can be here with you; obviously, I couldn't have done it, I was too busy talking to our CIA friends.'

*

Three days later

A young Filipino nurse entered Spiteri's room: 'Superintendent, this letter arrived for you'

'Thank you.'

Spiteri couldn't think who the letter would be from, and after reading it, she could barely think at all.

Thea,

I hope you are recovering well and not in too much pain. I'm sorry I was a little slow pulling the trigger, but at least I kept my vow of 'maybe saving your life one day.'

Please do not think ill of me. I did genuinely appreciate your friendship, and hope that one day we may meet again; possibly when this interminable war is over.

I'm not completely sure what you actually know about the terrible events that have taken place on your beautiful island recently, but I will inform you of two things:

Hank's father was Antoine Guerini. Sarti and Basti killed him over a dispute about money. Hank sought revenge. Being a 33°Grand Master Freemason, he knew that the JFK rifle was here on Malta and obtained permission to use it to kill Sarti Jnr and Basti Jnr 'to round the circle.' Getting the rifle wasn't a problem, but firing it was! Hank was hopeless. I was brought up on a farm in Tennessee; I could shoot before I could write. I killed Sarti Jnr….and Massa….but when I saw how you felt about Tizian, I decided to spare him. The car bomb changed everything. I hope you can forgive me.

The riddle of the rifle will forever remain just that: a riddle…a myth and a mystery. But I can assure you of one thing Thea….the gun is gone for good.

So, my dear Thea, this is goodbye……tell Jafar I was asking for him

Helen x

*

Spiteri lay back: *is it me that is mad….or them?* The phone in her Private Room buzzed.

'Hello, who's this?'

'Thea, it's Hunter…..sorry, Jafar. How are you?'

'Desolate.'

'You will go on…..there is no other option. Obviously, this is goodbye Superintendent, but I just wanted to confirm two things for you.'

'What would they be?'

'You have always been unsure of the cross-over of the various groups; the forming of a joint cabal?'

'Yes.'

'Do you have your laptop there?'

'Yes.'

'Google JFK April 27, 1961.'

'OK….and the second thing?'

'…..that there is a connection to Malta?'

'Yes.'

'When you have left the hospital and to help with your recovery, go to Casa Viana in Valletta….'

'The Masonic Lodge there?'

'Yes. From there drive 22 Km NNW. There you will come to the Ta Hagrat Temples. Read the historical notes there. Then drive 11 Km NNE to the Salina Park. Take a stroll there until you come to the JFK Memorial. Check the symbolism. Goodbye, Thea.'

Spiteri had already added the number of Kilometres together.

33

*

Adrianne Valetta wouldn't describe her work as pleasant or satisfying as such. To a certain extent she did enjoy inflicting the pain, watching the blood dripping, hearing the screams.

On the other hand, she hated feeding Michael Grech the food scraps; and hosing away his shit. It was bad enough doing it in the Cat & Dog Home in Floriana; never mind for the emasculated figure, pathetically beseeching forgiveness; that was manacled to the metal girder in front of her.

*

'Michael, Michael….you should be happy; you are the lucky one. In the past, I have merely castrated bastards like you and then released them. But now a Maltese heroine has been revealed; now I am going to look after you for 7 years….then release you; if you're still alive, of course.

*

Spiteri opened her laptop and connected to Google:

"For we are opposed around the world by a monolithic and ruthless conspiracy that relies primarily on covert means for expanding its sphere of influence--on infiltration instead of invasion, on subversion instead of elections, on intimidation instead of free choice, on guerrillas by night instead of armies by day. It is a system which has conscripted vast human and material resources into the building of a tightly knit, highly efficient machine that combines military, diplomatic, intelligence, economic, scientific and political operations. Its preparations are concealed, not published. Its mistakes are buried not headlined. Its dissenters are silenced, not praised. No expenditure is questioned, no rumour is printed; no secret is revealed."

John F. Kennedy's secret society speech on April 27, 1961

*

The cruise ship; Silver Whisper, which had left Valetta the previous day , was slowly making its way past Gozo at the start of a month-long Aegean Sea cruise. A woman, leaning over the port side of the liner, listened intently, and then smiled when she heard the nymph sing; this was the place. She raised the long leather case to her lips, and then discreetly let it slip into the sea. The same sea where, in the Mists of Time, a man named Ulysses would be saved by the daughter of a God.

Postscript

Fiction; Fact and 'the truth.'

Although "The Maltese Hunter" is a work of fiction; certain aspects of the story are considered by many to be fact, but is that the same thing as being true?

Not many people would consider Homer's "Odyssey" and "Iliad" as being true, but many of the people who feature in the stories did exist, and the fabled city of Troy [Hisarlik in modern day Turkey] is still there for all to see. Does this mean that Ulysses and Calypso existed? Probably not; but that wouldn't stop someone who was so-minded from "re-enacting" the scenario.

I'm stressing this point, as I feel it is important to beware of assuming that any particular version of a story is fact or true; and that view is what has allowed me to look at the JFK assassination with an open-mind. [Hopefully.]

However, the following issues are indeed true; and can be verified by a little research if so desired:

Perhaps the most pertinent example of this in "The Maltese Hunter" being that the chain of events and names leaked to Spiteri for her research into the JFK assassination by the fictional character: "Hunter" did indeed take place in the lead-up to the assassination of President Kennedy in 1963. I did not make these up; they happened and are on record. Any police officer in the world; including Spiteri!; would consider the amount of things that were dismissed as "coincidence" in the CIA-led investigations into the shootings, as laughable.

The fact alone, that Allen Dulles, CIA Director, who was dismissed by Kennedy for his attempted cover-up and lies concerning the disastrous Bay of Pigs operation; sat on the Warren Commission; [along with future President

Gerald Ford who would go on to 'Pardon' E Howard Hunt].…..which concluded that there was "no cover-up" surrounding the CIA's investigations into Kennedy's death is beyond parody.

*

Rifles, bullets and Fairy Tales

1.   The rifle found in the Texas Book Depository, and purported to be the one used by Oswald to kill Kennedy; was sent the day after the shooting to the FBI for examination.…Oswald's prints were NOT found on the gun. A couple of days later; while under intense questioning by the Press about the "lone gunman" story, Dallas DA Henry Wade announced that: "We have his fingerprints on the gun!" The next day the gun was ferried back to Dallas and taken to the Miller Funeral Home in Fort Worth, Texas. Two FBI officers took the gun and placed Oswald's dead fingers on the butt. The Director of the Miller Funeral Home; Paul Groody, was questioned and gave the statement above. It is 'On Record'; but it was dismissed by the Warren Commission as being irrelevant.

2.   Arlen Spector, the Warren Commission's 'magic-bullet' conspiracy theorist; went on to become an extremely high-profile Senator. However, this so-called 'magic bullet' was a high-velocity piece of ammunition while the Mannli-

cher-Carcano rifle that was supposedly used in the assassination is a low-velocity weapon, incapable of shooting this type of ammunition. Beyond this, the Mannlicher-Carcano is a piece of garbage weapon, costing less than twenty dollars, including the price of the scope. Several attempts at reconstructing the scenario put forward by the Warren Commission; using top military personnel, have resulted in not one of the marksmen being able to reproduce what Oswald is supposed to have achieved: and he was no top marksman according to his military records.

3.   Why no bullet marks on the car? There was. Carl Renas, Head of Security for the Ford Motor Company, was instructed to drive the car personally, under guard, to a specialist company called Hess & Eisenhart of Cincinnati. During the journey, Renas noticed several 'primary strikes' not 'fragments' holes the most noticeable being one 'on the windscreen's chrome moulding strip.' This would show the shot came from in front of the car; not behind. H & E replaced the strip and Renas was 'advised' by the secret service to "keep your mouth shut."

*

Apparently very unlucky people indeed

The only Catholic on the Warren Commission was Hale Boggs. When Boggs began to speak openly about the truthfulness of the findings, he soon found himself in a plane crash. His body was never found and he was declared dead.

In his book: "Crossfire: The Plot that killed Kennedy" Jim Marrs writes: "In the three-year period which followed the murder of President Kennedy and Lee Harvey Oswald, 18 material witnesses died — six by gunfire, three in motor accidents, two by suicide, one from a cut throat, one from a karate chop to the neck, five from natural causes." A mathematician concluded that the odds of this happening in a time-frame of Nov 1963 – Feb 1967 [date book published] were 100,000 TRILLION to 1.

These kind of figures were then substantiated by Roberts & Armstrong in their 1993 book: "JFK: The Dead Witnesses" where the figure had risen to 115 between Nov 1963 and Aug 1993.

*

The Israeli Connection

The plot line in the book, where it's asserted that Israel / Ben Gurion issued the order to kill

Kennedy; is just that, a plot line. The two pieces of back-plot, however, are true.

1. David Ben-Gurion: his birth name was indeed: David Gruen; and he was born on Oct 16, 1886, in Poland. His father; Victor Gruen was the leader of the "Lovers of Zion": a movement that captured the imagination of the oppressed Jewish peoples of Eastern Europe by preaching for a return to their original homeland of Israel. David Ben-Gurion felt that the first step in this process was to settle in Palestine, and this he did in 1906.

2. In May 1948 the State of Israel was established. David Ben-Gurion became Prime Minister and Minister of Defense. In 1954, the "Lavon Affair": which resulted in Israeli sabotage of U.S. properties in Egypt was generally regarded as a Ben Gurion inspired initiative. In June 1963 Ben Gurion unexpectedly resigned for un-named 'personal reasons' but, in reality, because JFK vehemently opposed Israel's desire to have nuclear weapons; and blocked any relevant supplies into Israel. After the assassination, the "Israel sympathiser" Lyndon Johnson, became President of USA and lifted all such importation restraints on Israel.

Convictions

The list of people convicted for having any involvement at all in the assassination of JFK isn't very long. In fact, there is no-one on it at all.

Incredibly only 1 person was even charged with involvement. His name was Clay Shaw [for those of you who have seen the Oliver Stone film: "JFK" may remember the excellent performance from Tommy Lee Jones who played the part of Shaw]

The evidence against Shaw was weak and the jury took only 2 hours to acquit him. Clay Shaw was a Knight of Malta.

Even more incredibly, E Howard Hunt, who made a deathbed confession of his part in the murder: was pardoned by.......former Warren Commission member, and future President, Gerard Ford! As they say in my hometown of Glasgow: "you couldn't make it up."

Finally, the JFK / Malta connection:
Interested parties did indeed erect a JFK Memorial, and it is in the Salinas Park near St Paul's Bay and is there for anyone to visit at any time.

Signs and symbols are there to decipher for anyone who can "see"...........

..........don't believe me? Go & look for yourself.

Bibliography

Unfortunately, many of the sources / information I've used in putting this story together came from the Internet and, such is the nature of that source, a lot of the postings aren't accredited.

However, I have tried hard to make sure that I have only included hard facts i.e. dates; places; people etc and I have used Accreditation below where I can.

Note: To listen to the JFK "Secret Society" speech…………..go to my website:
www.paulvincentlee.com

***

JFK: The Last Dissenting Witness
Jean Hill-Pelican Publishing
JFK: The Dead Witnesses
Craig Roberts
Consolidated Press
Crossfire: The Plot that killed Kennedy
James Marrs
KFK: Conspiracy of Silence
Charles Crenshaw
Penguin Books   the USA
Profiles in Conspiracy from JFK to George Bush:
Col James Gritz   Lazarus Publishing
First Hand Knowledge   Robert Morrow
Shapolsky Publishers
Vietnam: Why did we go? : Avro Manhattan
Chick Publications
JFK, The CIA, Vietnam and The Plot to Assassinate John F Kennedy   L Fletcher Prouty
Carol Publishing
The Men Who Killed Kennedy Stephen Rivele
Bloody Treason   Noel Twyman
Freemasonry in Malta   Wikipedia [various]
The Knights of Malta: The Real Truth   Wikipedia [various]

About the Author

The Maltese Orphans is an Agenda Bookstores Top 10 Crime Thriller Bestseller.

The Inspector Thea Spiteri Crime Series; set on the beautiful Mediterranean Island of Malta, exposes the underbelly of Paradise…..and enthrals Mystery & Thriller Fans Worldwide.

Visit: www.paulvincentlee.com : to download your FREE copy.

Lightning Source UK Ltd.
Milton Keynes UK
UKOW02f0340120117
291920UK00002B/9/P